DEEP FRIED TROUBLE

A Eugeena Patterson Mystery
Book 1

Tyora Moody

Deep Fried Trouble
A Eugeena Patterson Mystery, Book 1

Copyright © 2013 by Tyora Moody

Deep Fried Trouble is a work of fiction. Names, characters, places and incidents either are products of the author's imagination or are used fictitiously. Any resemblance to actual persons, living or dead, events, or locales is entirely coincidental.

Published by Tymm Publishing LLC
701 Gervais Street, Suite 150-185
Columbia, SC 29201
www.tymmpublishing.com

Cover Design: TywebbinCreations.com
Cover Illustration: CinnamonSaturday.com
Editing: TheJStandard.com

This book is dedicated to my mentors who have shaped me to become the woman I am today.

1

I should've turned around and gone back into the house as soon as I saw him. That would've been really silly since he'd already spotted me.

Eugeena Patterson, what's wrong with you? Get it together, woman.

I took a peek at my neighbor again. A quiver started in my stomach as I walked down the stone pathway in front of my home. The change of life had already paid a visit so I certainly couldn't blame my hormones for making my knees turn to jelly. More than likely my anxiousness had to do with being a widow almost three years. The loneliness of my home, once occupied by a family of five, had grown claustrophobic. Being officially retired, only a few days ago, after thirty years of service as a social studies teacher didn't help matters. All this free time on my hands made me act peculiar.

I couldn't believe that at my age, with three grown children and now three grandbabies, I had become infatuated with some man. An old one. But not bad looking, as far as I can tell with my new bifocals.

If only he wouldn't be looking at me.

Over the shrubbery that separated our property, Amos Jones waved at me. What could I do but be neighborly? I plastered a smile on my face and waved back.

Lord, please don't let me say anything crazy. So often I ended up feeling like I'd just put one of my size nine feet in my mouth.

With as much tact as I could, I smoothed my Patterson Family Reunion shirt around my hips, which didn't outline my rolls anymore. *Praise the Lord!*

One good thing about walking, I'd lost thirty pounds. My steps even felt lighter. I never had an hourglass figure mind you, but at least my pants weren't riding up between my thighs. That would have been too embarrassing.

Sure enough as I reached the sidewalk, Amos drove his lawn mower alongside me. The way he grinned, one would've thought his mode of transportation resembled a shiny red sports car. Men and their toys, especially the ones with wheels.

My impression of him remained the same as the first time I saw him over a year ago. He reminded me of Harry Belafonte. One of those men who managed to look more distinguished with age.

Now me? At fifty-nine, I looked nothing at all like the younger version of myself. Not that I was ever a beauty queen.

"How ya doing this morning, Mr. Amos?" My cheeks burned from grinning. "You got your grass looking all good, as usual." My right eyelid started to twitch. I hoped he didn't think I was batting my eyelashes.

I wasn't. The sun's rays had thrown an awful glare on my glasses. I positioned my hand against my forehead.

"Good mornin', Eugeena." Amos tipped his straw hat. That hat had probably seen better days. It curled up around Amos' balding head, fitting like a worn baseball glove. Little tuffs of white hair peeked out around the sides and the back. Amos must've handled a tractor at some point in his life. Those denim overalls spoke farm boy to me.

But his deep brown eyes mirrored a sophistication that defied the look he had going.

I shook my head, realizing those same eyes were gazing back at me with a puzzled expression. *Focus, Eugeena.* I cleared my throat, "Did you say something?"

"I said I see you're out for your morning walk."

He'd noticed.

"Yes, I got to manage this sugar," I said, thinking about the day a year before when my worst fear came to light. The day my doctor told me I had diabetes. Old folks liked to call it sugar. There was nothing sweet about the diagnosis. Since my husband's passing and now with an empty nest, I'd taken eating alone to a whole new level.

Amos commented, "Keep it up. You'll be fine. Hey, I see your grass needs attention. Wouldn't take me long to fix it up real nice for you."

My middle child, Cedric, lived nearby but he didn't cut the grass with any consistency. I knew I could've pulled out Ralph's old lawn mower, but I hated grass. My nose tickled from the freshly cut clippings stuck to the sidewalk and Amos' lawn mower.

Before I could protest, Amos crossed over from his front yard into mine. I leapt out of the way and threw my hand up to thank him. I guess this meant I was going to have to invite him over for a meal.

He looked like a fried chicken man to me. Of course, I needed to adjust my recipe a little bit. I already killed one man with my cooking.

I certainly didn't want to give Mr. Amos any ideas though. The poor man's wife hadn't been dead quite a year. Most men couldn't make it without a woman. I wasn't sure I wanted to be the missing piece in someone else's old puzzle.

My mind whirred with so many thoughts I hadn't realized I'd walked the opposite direction from my usual route. That Amos got my mind all off track.

Not a problem. I would just have to deal with the steep hill ahead. My body wouldn't be happy, but I did have another thirty pounds to lose.

Our neighborhood, known as Sugar Creek, was older than most of the new developments here in North Charleston. Many houses were brick, but most were wooden, their architectural style dating back to the mid-1940s. Most homes were two stories, fit with a garage or a carport. Large oaks covered with Spanish moss lined the street, but some trees were destroyed decades before, thanks to Hurricane Hugo.

I increased my pace, feeling the tension in the back of my calves as I climbed the hill. In a few hours the sun would be roasting. June arrived a few days before, breathing hot air down our necks like some irate dragon.

4

At the top of the hill, a white house came into view. Despite the weathered exterior, it still looked beautiful, surrounded by the oaks and magnolia trees.

I used to visit the occupant of the house, but we, that is Mary Fleming and I had long since parted ways. Our exchange was always awkward. I would wave hello and she'd wave back. We would display weak smiles. The kind of smile, where you barely showed any teeth or just let your mouth curve slightly upward. As soon as I passed her house, my steps seemed to grow more difficult the farther I walked away.

My chest heaved from having to climb that stupid hill. I thanked the Lord I'd reached the top.

I didn't have long to rejoice about my victory when something ran alongside my line of vision. The brown and white blur not only romped next to me, but was barking its little head off too. I slowed down and looked over at Mary's Corgi.

"Porgy." Yes, Mary named that dog after the character from *Porgy and Bess*. The name always seemed odd to me. The little noisemaker's round tummy shook as he waddled beside me. He should have been named Porky instead. "What are you doing outside?"

One thing I knew about Mary, she guarded Porgy with her life. She'd never let that pooch out of her sight and he certainly wouldn't have been in the front yard.

I peered through the fence a little closer. Something wasn't right with Porgy's fur. The normally well-groomed dog looked matted and just plain dirty. "Porgy, you been into some mud hole. Mary is going to have a fit." I couldn't keep walking. Besides, my legs were killing me.

This must have been a sign from the Lord. Mary and I had held onto our grudges long enough. It wouldn't hurt to have a real conversation for a change. Amos and I weren't the only widowed folks on this street. Poor Mary had lost not only her spouse, but her only child five years ago in a horrible car accident. Sometimes I felt like the Lord was leading me to rekindle the friendship. I dealt with loneliness, but my children and grandchildren came to visit me. Poor Mary, she'd lost everyone dear to her and had become a bit of a hermit.

Porgy barked his little head off as I unlatched the white fence door. Yes, a white picket fence. This house had all the elements of a perfect home down to the wrap-around porch and shutters. Most houses down the hill had bits and pieces, but none of the houses, including mine, spoke grandness like Mary's.

Once inside the fence, I followed the erratic dog around to the back. "Mary?" Around the side of the house, daylilies ranging from pink to yellow were in full bloom. The woman had always been a master gardener. I tried, but can't say I had much of a green thumb.

This really felt strange. I hadn't been in the Fleming's backyard in years. Not much had changed. Same wrought iron furnishings with overstuffed green cushions. The big gas grill sat covered on the side. I remembered when Mary planted the hydrangeas and azaleas along the deck's sides.

It was beautiful back there. Quiet.

Too quiet.

The boards of the deck creaked as I placed my weight on the steps. Since the blinds were pulled back, I could see clearly through the patio sliding door. I tapped the glass and shouted, "Mary, are you in there? Porgy is outside about to have a fit."

The dog yapped, sounding more like a chimpanzee as he ran in circles. My goodness, poor little fellow. How long had Mary left him outside?

I cupped my hands to my face and peered inside. On the other side of the door, the kitchen sparkled. No. Really. I could see the shine from where I stood. Old Mary was somewhat of a neat freak and she loved her stainless steel appliances. I'd always thought she would've been perfect in a Mr. Clean commercial or something.

I shifted my eyes around the kitchen. I froze. Now mind you, a glass of water sitting on the counter shouldn't produce alarm. For some reason, my mind recollected every tidbit I knew about my former friend. The Mary I knew wouldn't just leave a glass sitting on her granite countertop. After you drank from it, you rinsed the glass and put it in the dishwasher. My own children were familiar with the routine whenever they visited the Fleming's home.

Next to me, poor Porgy whimpered. I walked to the other glass door and again cupped my hand around my face.

"Sweet Jesus." I stepped backwards.

Porgy yelped.

"I'm sorry. I didn't mean to step on your tail." I also wished I hadn't seen what I saw.

The woman I once counted as a close friend lie on her kitchen floor. Her blank stare seemed to beg for help. Oh, but I couldn't help her.

2

It was a good thing I hadn't eaten breakfast yet. It would've ended up on Mary's patio floor, which I'm sure the crime scene investigators wouldn't have appreciated. I scooped up poor Porgy as fast as I could, and took off running like a mad woman back down the hill. I know I scared poor Amos. He'd looked up and almost collided with the boxwoods shrubbery bordering my property. Amos cut off the lawn mower and rushed toward me.

I grabbed his arm. "It's Mary. I think she's dead."

Amos whipped out his cell phone and punched in some numbers.

I plunked the dog and myself down on my front porch steps. For the next thirty minutes, official looking vehicles ascended the hill. It wasn't long before my neighbors ventured out of their homes, probably disturbed by all the sirens.

I, on the other hand, was disturbed for another reason. I would never have the chance to make up for lost time with Mary. I felt so many times the Lord drawing me to be the bigger person, after all, I did make the biggest fuss. Now all was lost.

Porgy sat by my side, panting his little heart out. His black eyes looked so sad; I could barely stand to look at him. I placed my hands over my eyes to block out my surroundings, wishing I could curl up in a ball.

All of a sudden Porgy started barking. I moved my hands from my face to find a person staring at me from across the street.

Wayne Goodman.

I watched that boy grow up. Really, I couldn't call him a boy, more like a man who never quite grew up. Trouble followed Wayne like a cat set on a mouse's trail. In and out of prison, so I heard, I knew he was in his late thirties, around the age of my youngest son. Other than occupying his deceased mother's home, he didn't seem to be up to much of anything with his life.

A few months before, we had a string of burglaries. In my opinion, the crimes really started when Wayne showed back up. I could be a little on the judgmental side, but that boy seemed a bit too old to be wearing his pants slung down round his hips. What happened to wearing belts? And someone please give me some clippers so I can have at that head of hair. Half braided, half afro. *Make up your mind, mister.*

"Eugeena. Eugeena."

I took my eyes off Wayne to catch Louise Hopkins shuffling down the sidewalk from her house, which was on the other side of mine. If I had to say seventy-year old Louise was my oldest friend in the world. Her once blond hair had turned completely white. She was the spunkiest white woman I'd ever met.

We didn't too much like each other at first. Funny, how God worked through an armor of fears and stereotypes to form a friendship.

I stood. "Louise, you better slow down. We don't need you breaking your hip."

"Oh please. Don't nothing hold me back. What about you? I heard you found Mary."

How did she hear so fast? I wasn't trying to figure it out either. Louise had probably lived in Sugar Creek the longest, back during a time when the neighborhood wasn't quite as diverse. One time she even told me her great great-granddaddy owned a plantation right here in Charleston. That turned out to be one interesting conversation.

Anyhow, there was nothing Louise didn't know. She'd outlived two husbands and two children. The one child she had left, William, was traipsing off somewhere in the Louisiana bayou or was it the Florida Everglades. I couldn't keep up with Louise's stories of her son's adventures. I rarely saw the man and often wondered if ole Louise wasn't telling some fibs every now and then.

"Well, what happened?" Louise leaned on my porch railing trying to catch her breath.

Porgy yipped and yapped.

"Shush, little dog. It'll be okay."

"You got Mary's dog there. That little mutt must really like you. I'm a cat person myself. Always will be."

Porgy growled. Smart little thing. He even knew when

someone insulted him.

I picked up the dog and he nestled under my arm. "I had to do something. He would've been in the way of..."

"The cops. Eugeena, there were so many cars heading towards Mary's house. You know I had a bad feeling. We talked about this the other night, remember?"

"Yeah." I wish Louise hadn't reminded me. Louise started the neighborhood watch program years ago and was still in shock she had asked me to head it up. I didn't know anything about running a watch. Sticking my nose out the window from time to time to make note of suspicious characters seemed to be the only thing I knew to do.

By now, several neighbors were swarming in from every direction like ants at a church picnic, coming to invade my front yard. As the official president of the Sugar Creek Neighborhood Watch, people needed me to keep them informed. I hope no one thought I was going to invite them in for coffee and donuts. I was in no mood to be hospitable.

I discovered my former friend's dead body and I might not ever be the same. *Sweet Jesus, help me.*

3

I nodded at Wayne as he approached. Then, I stood and hugged Tamara Robertson, one of the new neighbors. She was such a petite little thing. Her deep chocolate skin had not a single blemish. It really was hard to tell if she was 18 or 30. As far as I knew, she was a newlywed because she mentioned her husband, Melvin, all the time.

"Miss Eugeena, are you okay?" Tamara's brown eyes were wide, staring at Porgy.

Porgy was barking and running in circles like he was having a doggy breakdown.

I shook my head and turned towards Tamara. "Honey, I'm fine." I stepped away from Tamara and looked at my neighbors. "You know all of you didn't have to come over to check on me."

Towering over Tamara, Carmen Alpine stepped forward with her hands on her hips. "Miss Eugeena, you have to tell us what happened!"

Built like an Amazon woman, Carmen looked like she could take a man down. I forgot what she did for a living, but she certainly took care of her body. Voluptuous, but definitely fit like that singing gal, Beyoncé, and with all the attitude of a Cleopatra Jones, she was not a sister to pick a fight with that's for sure. Her eyebrow shot up as she continued. "When we met at your house last week, we were talking about burglaries, now we got a murder. I thought this was supposed to be a decent neighborhood."

Folks started up with the protests.

"Now hold on, people." I looked around at all the faces in my yard, conscious again of the hot temperature. Sweat poured down every crevice in my body. Not a good feeling. Understandably people were scared. But I was not the one to be interrogated. If anything I needed to know what these people knew.

Anybody in this neighborhood could have easily walked to Mary's house and killed her. I had no idea why since the woman barely socialized with people. Still from what I knew from watching *Perry Mason* and *Murder She Wrote*, Mary might have known her killer. Somebody close by could have watched her activities, which were probably pretty routine since she didn't leave the house often. "How did all of you hear this information? Who told you somebody died?"

Everyone was quiet and looked around at each other.

Wayne's deep voice broke the awkward silence. "I don't know about anyone else, but the way you came tearing down the hill a while ago, I knew something really bad happened."

Was I screaming or something? I know pure terror had engulfed my soul.

Louise sat down on my step. "All those sirens gave me a clue. Looked like a scene from a cop show. Plus some detective has been around asking questions."

Carmen interrupted, "Yeah. Totally took me by surprise this morning. How did she die? Was it a gun? I always tell people you need something to defend yourself with. I got...."

"Carmen, that's enough. Y'all, I don't know any more than what you know. I saw a disturbing scene this morning and quite frankly I'm too shook up to really talk now."

Tears sprang to my eyes. Oh Lord, why did you take Mary? My sorrow swooped on me like a hawk going after its prey. I sat back down on my step, the hard brick work pressed into my thighs.

Porgy reminded me of his presence by licking my arms. *Ew!* Sweat and doggy spit. Okay, we were going to have to set some ground rules with that canine and I needed some AC. The humidity had encased my heavy frame like a warm blanket. But first I needed to run my neighbors out my yard. "Y'all, it's getting hot out here. We'll talk later."

There were a few grumbles, mainly from Louise. She hadn't gotten her scoop, but I knew she didn't want to stay out in the sun despite her need to be in the know. Carmen and Tamara talked as they walked out the gate. Wayne slinked off, following behind the two women.

The little Corgi started barking again like he owned my porch. I looked towards the sidewalk to see what had his attention this time. A woman dressed in khaki pants and a white shirt stood at the edge of my property talking to Amos. He must have sensed me staring because he glanced over. Our eyes met.

The woman turned, taking note of where I sat and walked

away from Amos.

I stood. Up close, I could see her red hair was pinned at the top of her head, but some sprigs had escaped and were stuck to her freckled face.

"Ma'am, how are you doing? I understand you found the body?"

"Yes."

"Can you tell me a little about what you found?" The woman flipped a page in her pad and poised her pen. "Were you going to visit the deceased this morning?"

The deceased had a name. "Yes. I mean no. I was on my morning walk and noticed Porgy here." I pointed to the little dog who sat looking up at the woman with an inquisitive face. I had some questions of my own. "By the way, who are you?"

The woman looked sheepish. "I'm sorry." She reached in her pocket and pulled out a badge. "I'm Detective Sarah Wilkes. Now you said you were walking and the dog was out. Why was this unusual?"

"If you knew Mary, you'd know she'd never let this dog out of her sight."

"He seems pretty friendly with you. Did you go over there a lot?"

"Well, no. I did when she first got him. He's about five years old. I guess he remembers me."

"So, you hadn't visited with Mary in five years?"

Here we go. "We didn't visit with each other as often. Mary and I sort of grew apart." That's all she needed to know.

"I see. So, you thought it was strange that the dog was out. What did you do next?"

16

"I called Mary's name several times. When she didn't answer, I walked all the way around to the back of the house. I thought maybe she was engrossed with the flowers and didn't notice Porgy was missing from her side."

"What did you see when you arrived?"

"I peeked in through the glass doors. I saw the glass of water on the counter. I guess that might not mean nothing, but Mary didn't like things lying around."

"She could have sat it there to check on something at the front part of the house."

"But she wouldn't have locked her dog out of the house. That also doesn't explain..."

I gulped. The image of Mary's face made me shudder.

"Are you alright, Mrs. Patterson? Do you have something else to share?"

"Yes. No. I'm fine."

"Are you sure?" The young woman cocked her eyebrow, and studied my face before speaking again. "Anyone we can contact for you?"

"I'm fine. Really."

"Can you think of anyone who might want to harm the deceased?"

There she goes again. The woman's name was Mary. "No. Mary really was more of a recluse since she'd lost her family years ago. She didn't bother anyone and nobody bothered her."

"So, she didn't have any tiffs with anyone. Sometimes people who live alone like that get annoyed easily."

The only disagreement I knew Mary had was with me. In

fact, most of the neighborhood knew. Sure, it was past history, but there were some folks who might decide to volunteer the past feud with the detective. I couldn't let that happen, so, I offered her my two cents. "There have been several burglaries lately. I'm not sure how long poor Porgy was outside, but suppose Mary ran into an intruder?"

"That's a possibility." The woman scratched down some notes and then snapped her pad closed. "The investigation is still early in the process. We can't verify if this was a robbery just yet, but thanks for the tip though." She reached inside her front pocket and handed me a card. "Just in case you think of something else, don't hesitate to give me a call."

"Thank you, Detective. I will."

Now more than ever I regretted being appointed the neighborhood association president. At the meeting a few weeks ago, we discussed the protocols to follow if we saw something suspicious. Even Wayne offered some tips. Apparently, that boy picked a few locks at some point in his life. This raised my suspicions about him even more.

Even if he was a thief, I couldn't quite picture him as a killer. I didn't want anyone in the neighborhood to fit that description.

How did I get this much responsibility on my shoulders? I'm retired.

I looked down at Porgy. "We're going to find out what happened to your mama. In the meantime, you need a place to stay."

I couldn't believe what I was doing. Boy, if Ralph was alive he'd thrown a fit. God had a way of working situations out. The least I could do for poor Mary was to take care of her most prized possession. I also needed to find out who took her life.

4

We patrolled Sugar Creek from my porch. Amos and I. Oh yeah, and little McGruff the Crime Dog. Porgy's ears shot up from time to time. With his tummy full of Kibbles 'n Bits, thanks to Amos, he seemed at peace despite being in a strange home. I wish I felt a bit peaceful.

My eyes wandered up the hill wondering what evidence the investigators had found. The card from Detective Wilkes sat near my phone in the hallway. Who knows? I might think of something else. I already knew sweet dreams wouldn't be visiting me.

It was still muggy even though the sun had dipped lower in the sky. Every once in a while a breeze caressed my skin. To keep us cool, I'd fixed some fresh brewed sweet tea. I said brewed not that powdered stuff. You can choke and die on that nasty concoction some folks liked to call tea.

I was still trying to get myself used to Splenda. It ain't half bad.

I kicked my foot to get the rocking chair to glide back and forth. The chairs were old, but comfortable. With a recent coat of white paint, thanks to my oldest son, the chairs looked brand new.

Amos still wore his denim overalls, but at least he'd retired his hat onto his knee. He looked content. I didn't want to disturb him, but I needed advice and he seemed like the logical place to start. Plus, it gave me a chance to actually talk to him about something besides the weather and the grass.

I knew he'd worked in law enforcement in some type of capacity. Today, he'd managed to get the necessary authorities to Mary's house in no time and seemed to be quite friendly with the crew traipsing around behind the crime tape.

"Amos, you know about the neighborhood association?"

"Yeah, the group is a good idea. Now more than ever. People are getting stranger and stranger."

Tell me about it. Signs of the times for sure. "I can't help but think how none of us helped poor Mary. What can we do to prevent this from happening again?" Better yet, I wanted to find the culprit. All afternoon I'd watched neighbors come and go. I didn't realize how many folks I didn't know. The neighborhood had changed, and now a new crop of young couples and their children lived here. A few retirees like me, Louise and Amos were scattered here and there.

Amos and his wife were from the crop of northern folks who chose to retire on the coast of South Carolina instead of Florida. Charleston was a town rich in history, some bad and some good.

Amos stopped rocking. "I'm still new here, has anything like this happened before in the neighborhood? I was reading the other day; North Charleston had been ranked the seventh-most dangerous city in the nation back in 2007. In recent years, the crime rate decreased. I believe we are around sixty-three now. That's a definite improvement."

"Yeah, I saw that list." I shivered. "Still Jesus must be coming back soon. The world has clearly lost it."

There were rumors about young men selling drugs out of their home. The house was three doors down from mine. Both young men waved when I passed by, but they did have an awful lot of folks in and out their house at night. They suddenly moved. Nobody knew where they went or where they came from.

Then, there are the robberies. Poor Annie Mae and Willie Mae Brown, the two sisters who lived a few doors down came home one night from playing bingo only to find many valuables stolen, including their television. For days those two old women couldn't stop talking about missing their stories. Now who would've thought the world would come to an end when you couldn't see your soap operas? Even though I was here during the day now, I still couldn't bring myself to get attached to television actors and their imaginary problems.

Now Dr. Phil. I can watch that man all day. He tells it like it is. Just the way I like it.

Amos held up his index finger. "You know what you need is to get some history. Police reports are public record you know."

I raised an eyebrow at Amos' suggestion. "Really? I know they have a database for sex offenders. Do I need to be checking all that out?" I can't believe the word sex came out of my mouth in front of this man. When he was alive, I don't think my own husband heard me say that word. Ever.

"If you want to make this neighborhood association stronger than those signs y'all got up and down the street, you need to know what you are up against."

"Can you help with some of this?"

Amos grinned. He still had all his teeth. They didn't appear to be dentures either. "I will be happy to help where I can."

That made me feel a tad bit better. I've wondered how Amos spent his retirement days in an empty house, a predicament I was still adjusting to myself. The more I thought about what happened to Mary, the more I started to fathom my own lonely state.

I had Cedric's steel baseball bat. But what good would that do me if someone walked in on me with a gun?

And Mary. I sucked in a breath. *Maybe I shouldn't leave that butcher block of knives sitting around on my kitchen counter.*

A noise broke through my worry session. I looked down at my feet where the dog laid. His eyes were closed tight. I listened. Well, Porgy was no guard dog that's for sure. That little mutt had the nerve to be snoring. We can't have that. I'm the only one who snores in my house. Sometimes I woke myself up.

I would lie awake for sure. Visions of murder and mayhem would assail me for the rest of the night.

"Eugeena." Amos had stopped rocking. "I believe you've got company."

Sure enough, a car had slowed down in front of my house. I know I needed to work on being more hospitable, but it was getting late in the day.

I eased my hips out of the rocking chair to get a better look at the vehicle. Dusk had arrived quickly, casting a reddish tone across the landscape. The car turned into my driveway. When I caught sight of the old Nissan Altima, I wasn't sure if I should shout for joy or slump in misery. My prodigal daughter had returned.

5

There would be no sleep tonight. Leesa Patterson, my youngest and only girl walked towards the porch holding what appeared to be a blanket. As her mother, I should have been happy to see her, especially since four months had passed since I saw her last. Oh, she called. She called when she needed me to wire money. Then, she'd forget about me.

Funny, that's how she was conceived. One night, I forgot how much I despised Ralph and I guess he remembered I was his wife. Nine months later, with two sons in high school, Leesa made her entrance. She'd always been good at surprises. Like showing up out of the blue.

"Hey Mama." Leesa looked behind her. "Kisha, say hello to Grandma."

I watched as a small hand snaked around Leesa's bare leg and then a head appeared. The large eyes looked up at me.

My little Kisha. I still felt she was a little small for a four year old. "Hey precious, come to Grandma."

Shyly stepping from behind her mother, Kisha smiled and then reached her arms up. I pulled her up into my arms and squeezed. Lord, how I missed this grandchild.

My oldest boy made sure his twin boys spent time with me. Both of those monsters made me lose my senses sometime, but I hated the quiet house even more after they left.

I stared at Leesa, who seem to be looking everywhere, but at my face. Something wrestled in the pit of my stomach. My poor stomach had experienced a lot in one day. I couldn't remember what I ate, which probably wasn't good for my blood sugar. Earlier the levels were normal. I did remember to do that much for myself. Got to take care of this body of mine. I've already failed it thus far.

Amos cleared his throat behind me. I whirled around embarrassed; I'd almost forgotten him. "Amos, you remember my daughter Leesa?" How could he? She doesn't come around that much.

"I do remember her. Nice to see you again." Amos stood and held out his hand.

Leesa cringed. Something in her arms squirmed. A little arm popped out of the blue blanket, and my heart skipped a beat.

"Leesa, who's this?"

My daughter turned her body to the side to show me an adorable little face. "Mama, this is Tyric."

"My baby brother," Kisha yelled.

All kinds of questions ran through my head. I know it had been sometime since I'd seen Leesa, but when was she pregnant with that baby? Why didn't she tell me? Who was the father?

Amos made a choking sound.

I wanted to choke my child. Instead of peppering her with questions, I turned around. "Amos, I guess this is goodnight. Thanks for talking with me."

He tipped his hat before placing it on his head. "My pleasure. Goodnight, ladies." I watched him walk away, wishing I could follow him home.

"Grandma, you have a dog now?" My precious granddaughter had discovered Porgy or rather vice versa. The dog wagged his tail and seemed delighted by all the attention he was receiving.

"Looks like it, sweetie pie. Let's go inside." I grabbed the little one by the hand and marched back towards the kitchen, making sure she washed her hands at the sink. Kisha, then made herself at home at the kitchen table, while I opened and closed cabinets. Finding plates, I put them on the table, ignoring my daughter until I could figure out what to say. Eating always helped. Or not.

My beautiful grandbaby, the one I knew about, gave me a crumb-covered smile as she gobbled the peanut butter and jelly sandwich I had made in apprehensive silence. I smiled back, feeling tension slightly release from my shoulders.

Then I focused on Leesa. I tried not to frown, but the spot between my eyebrows clinched up.

Leesa had the nerve to get pregnant with Kisha her senior year in high school. As much as this child struggled, why would she bring another child in this world? She just turned twenty-one a few months back and as hard as I tried to get her back in school, it was a closed subject.

I nodded my head towards Tyric. "I'm waiting for the explanation for this one."

"Mama…"

"A few weeks ago when you called crying about not being able to pay the rent, you couldn't have mentioned there was going to be a new mouth to feed. Even more so, why didn't you tell me before now? I'm your mother. I was there with you for the first one."

"I'm sorry. I wasn't sure."

"Chile, it wasn't like you hadn't been through this before." I looked over at Kisha, who sat next to me, now munching on a cookie. Her eyes traveled back and forth between me and her mother.

Leesa huffed, "Mama, we are just here for a few days. If you don't want us, I can leave right now."

There she goes twisting things around. That's not what I wanted. For your grown child to show up out of the blue and with an extra child, it didn't seem too much to have some questions answered.

"Don't be going all drama queen on me, Leesa Patterson. I asked you a question. And you know this house is always open to you."

The last time I saw Leesa it was just before Easter. Her weight went up and down like mine. Always wearing big shirts and baggy jeans, it would've never occurred to me to think she was pregnant. Fooled again. Four years ago, if it wasn't for the child complaining about stomach pain, I still wouldn't have imagined she'd been carrying Kisha all *that* time.

Somewhere along the way, my two sons must have worn me down. I missed the boat when Leesa came into this world. I was thirty-eight years old and I had the audacity to have a child fifteen years after the last one. By then, my students had grown more and more difficult each year. I was so tired, I couldn't wait until the day I would see retirement.

A wail started up from the little body in Leesa's arms. She tried to move him around in her arms and rock him, but with eyes tightly shut, mouth wide open, he wailed louder.

Porgy who had been sitting in the corner, ran under the table, and wrapped his self around my foot. Kisha reached her little arms around my waist, well at least as far as her arms could go. "Make him stop, Grandma."

"Let me hold him."

"Mama, I can handle this."

"I didn't say you couldn't. You look like you could use a break."

Without much coddling, Leesa held the hollering baby away from her as though he offended her and passed him to me. I cradled the baby in my arms, surprised by his small body.

A lullaby sprang forth from my lips. One I hadn't thought about in years. He was definitely a small little fellow, I estimated he couldn't be more than a month old. As I hummed, sang and hummed again, Tyric's beautiful brown eyes looked up at me in wonderment. He'd forgotten all about whatever ailed him.

Leesa looked under the table and frowned. "Mama, isn't that Mary's dog?"

"Oh no. I need to tell you."

"Tell me what?"

I shifted Tyric in my arms. "I found Mary." I checked Kisha. She seemed to be feeding Porgy something under the table. Cookies. That figured. I continued, "Someone *k-i-l-l-e-d* her." I didn't want to give my grandchild nightmares. I would have enough for both of us.

"What? No!"

"If I hadn't seen it with my own eyes, I guess I would be saying the same thing."

Leesa wilted in the seat like she did as a teenager. "This is all too much. I'm so tired of everything."

"Tired of everything?" I stared at my youngest child. *What else had my baby girl gotten into now?*

Leesa keeps her eyes on the kitchen table. She quietly answers, "Just tired, that's all."

Something was wrong, but I didn't need to know tonight. At least she came home, whatever the trouble this time. She was safe with me. "Do you want something to eat?"

"I'm fine, Mama." Leesa stood. "Is my room still the same?"

"Nothing has changed."

"I think I need to lie down for awhile."

It was barely eight o' clock. She needed to lie down. Let's see I'm about to turn sixty and she was only twenty-one. *Why is she so tired? And where was she going, leaving me with these children?*

I had two mysteries, one started with death, the other with life.

30

We were going to get some answers.

6

Sleep held me hostage. I knew Sunday was the Lord's day. Second Sunday, in fact. My day to usher. I couldn't wait to enter Missionary Baptist Church, because after finding Mary the day before, I definitely needed a word from the Lord.

A sweet, sweet spirit hovered around me. I inhaled and began my morning session with Jesus. It had taken me a long time to learn that going to church wasn't all about what I could get from the Lord. Prayer was a time to bless the Lord. Praise Him.

I hummed, "Oh how I love Jesus, Oh..."

A baby howled from somewhere deep in the house. I almost called out Ralph's name, but then I remembered he hadn't lain in that bed in years. I sat up and rubbed my eyes. Whose baby was that? Wide awake, my brain started to assemble facts.

Ralph, Jr. and his wife would be visiting with the twins soon. My other son, Cedric, had no grandkids yet. Neither was he married. He worried me sometime.

A creature scrambled up the side of my bed. I jolted at seeing black button eyes. Now it all dawned on me. "Porgy, who told you to be on my bed?" I know for sure I'd put that dog in the other room.

The discovery of Mary's body came tumbling back into my memory. The last time I saw Mary alive was Mother's Day weekend. I ushered that Sunday too. I couldn't help but notice the sadness in her eyes. Who would've known I would never see her again?

I still couldn't get over that furry creature sneaking in my bed. He must've slept beside Mary.

I ain't that lonesome.

As I pushed my feet into my bunny slippers, I remembered I needed to talk to my daughter. Her little booger interrupted my talk time with Jesus, which I really needed. Surely, I can get an explanation about my new grandchild.

Porgy started barking.

"Don't you start that mess. One howling baby is all I can't take right now."

"Leesa." I grabbed my robe and wrapped it around my frame. The terry robe was old and tattered. The belt fit a tad bit better around my waist than it used to. That was encouraging since it wasn't too long ago I couldn't close the robe over my gut.

It was one of the few things left that Ralph purchased for me. It was one of my favorite pieces of clothing. That man had brought me a lot of pain, but thankfully God brought Ralph to his senses. I will always be grateful for the last few years we had together before another heart attack took his life. I treasured my three children and grandchildren even more.

"Leesa, what's wrong? Is everything okay?" Before I traveled down the hallway good, a small body collided into me. "Kisha, what's wrong?" The little girl had tears streaming down her face. She clung to my robe, unloosening my neatly tied belt. "Girl, you can't hang onto me like that. You and me are going to hit this floor." Porgy jumped up and down, circling both of us.

Can you say catastrophe in progress?

I pried away the tiny fingers wedged into my waist and gazed down at the tear-stained face. "Honey, what's wrong with you? Where's your mama?"

"I ...I ...I don't know...Grandma," Kisha wailed louder.

I reached down and picked up the distraught child. Making my way down the hall, I heard the baby screaming at the top of his little lungs.

This didn't feel right to me. Not at all. Maybe Leesa stepped out for a few minutes.

I placed Kisha on the bed next to her brother. Little Tyric pumped his little legs up and down.

"Alright, little mister. No need to have a temper tantrum." He certainly acted like a Patterson. I picked up the crying baby. "Kisha, did your mama say where she was going?"

No response.

With her head hanging down, the little girl sucked on her finger and sniffled. I placed my hand on her forehead. It was warm to the touch. "Did mama say she was going to the store?"

No answer.

My stomach started to flutter and it wasn't because I craved my morning baked cheese grits. Now that recipe was worth finding. I've had a love affair with cheese all my life. Cheese crackers, cheese doodles, cheeseburgers... well at least my new food plan wasn't turning out to be such a tragedy.

I rubbed my hands over Kisha's ratty braids. We needed to do something about that hair. A good shampooing was in the works, but for now, I needed to know where my daughter took off. "Kisha, baby you feeling okay? What did mama say?"

"Don't know."

"You don't know. Well, did you see her when she left?" Now this child had to know something.

"No."

I wasn't feeling too good about this situation. Leesa had the nerve to get up and leave these children. She did say she needed to stay a few days. What was it that she said last night? *I'm so tired of everything.*

Then, it dawned on me. Was she talking about her and the kids or just the kids? Now wait a minute, that girl promised me we would talk in the morning. Well, it was morning. Where was she?

Panic started to rise up in my stomach. Sweat popped out from body. Did they have bags? Over in the corner sat a pink *Dora the Explorer* bookbag.

"Kisha, you want a bubble bath?"

Her eyes lit up. "Lots of bubbles."

"Yes, lots of bubbles. Show me where your clothes are. Let's pick out an outfit."

Children. One minute they were crying, the next, they were running around happy as a skunk. Kisha raced ahead of me. Tyric looking around at the walls and seemed to have quieted down, now that he was being held.

I glanced at the clock. Already ten o'clock. Where did the time go? I needed to get myself ready for church this morning. Leesa, you better get back here soon. I certainly couldn't usher and keep up with these two today.

When I arrived in the Leesa's bedroom, Kisha was bent over a large blue duffel bag. I recognized the bag being on Leesa's shoulder last night. Kisha pulled out several clothes entwined together in a ball. Either Leesa was in a hurry or never learned how to fold clothes.

Kisha pulled out clothes that appeared to be her size, leaving others in a pile on the floor. It didn't look like any of those clothes on the floor fit an adult.

"That girl, I know she didn't."

"Grandma, I didn't do anything."

"Honey, I was just talking out loud." *About your sorry mama.*

I walked over, picked the bag off the floor and sat it on the bed. While balancing little Tyric on my hip, I decided to unpack the clothes so they wouldn't be wrinkled to death.

When I get my hands on that girl.

I tell you there's nothing like being bamboozled by your own child. I always said I was not going to be one of those grandmothers caught raising their grandkids. She better have some diapers for the little one in the diaper bag over in the corner.

I picked up the diaper bag. There were diapers. A pacifier. Bibs.

"Grandma, I want to wear this?"

I glanced at a bright pair of yellow pants and a pink top.

"That looks good, baby."

I pulled out a half a dozen diapers from the bag.

"What in the world?"

Were my eyes playing tricks on me?

My daughter better get back here soon. That girl had some serious explaining to do about the contents of this diaper bag.

7

I stared into the bag with a million scenarios going through my mind. The phone rang from the other room. *It better be her.* I transferred Tyric to my other hip, so I could grab the phone for my good ear. I'd been meaning to get my left ear checked out for weeks.

"Leesa, where you at?"

"Mom?"

Oops. The deep voice on the other line was a child of mine, but not the one I needed to be talking to.

"Junior, honey, how are you?"

"What's that sister of mine up to now?"

"Calm down. Leesa came by last night with the kids?"

Ralph Jr. remained quiet for a few seconds. "Did you say kids?"

Oops again. Tyric seemed to be a surprise for the whole family.

"When did she have another kid?"

I felt faint. I did not need that, but I needed to take my medicine. "Ralph, look I need to get off the phone and get ready for church."

"Mom, do I need to come down there?"

"No. You stay with your own family, mister. I don't need your help here."

"If I know my sister, she's probably up to no good."

"Ralph Jr." I really didn't need my oldest, control freak son to echo my deepest fear. "I'll talk to you later. Say hello to Judy and the boys for me."

I slammed the phone down before he could get another word in. Junior meant well. He was so much like me, except he handled things with the fixit attitude that God gifted to men. I'd taken all I could take of that same attitude from Ralph, Sr. who was lying six feet under.

"Grandma, I'm ready for my bubble bath."

"Okay, baby. That's a good idea." I placed Kisha in the tub and then undressed Tyric and bathed him at the sink. By the time I got both of the children towel-dried, I was steaming mad at my daughter.

The doorbell interrupted the tirade going on in my mind.

I grabbed Tyric, who at least was fully dressed and stomped down the stairs. I yanked the front door open, "Leesa, you better…"

My facial muscles sagged, switching from anger to confusion. This was not the person I expected. "Amos, what are you doing here?" I'd been up for hours, but suddenly became aware of the gritty texture in my mouth. I hadn't brushed my teeth, and my ratty robe was practically hanging open. I didn't have anything to give Amos an eyeful of, but I knew I must have looked like an old hag.

Amos cleared his throat. "Well, I thought I would check to see if you were heading to Missionary Baptist today."

Okay, now that made me smile.

"I tell you what, hold this fellow?" I passed Tyric over to Amos. Both males looked wide-eyed at the exchange.

"I don't know anything about babies," Amos stuttered.

"You two will be just fine. Come on here." I looked at the grandfather clock in the foyer. "If you could do me a favor, I promise you I will fix you the best fried chicken you'd ever had in your life."

Amos grinned back. "Sounds good to me."

"Grandma, look I dressed myself."

I spun around. My precious Kisha looked like a precious mess. Did stripes and polka dots even go together? That's alright. She could get away with being cute. We were late. "Baby girl, sit here with Mr. Amos, while I get ready."

I bounded up the stairs with more energy than my years could handle. I'd noticed Porgy had made himself comfortable on my bed again. Whatever. I had no time to fool with a dog.

Before I headed to the bathroom, I stopped in the guest room and grabbed the diaper bag. I shut the door and sat on the commode. With a bit of trepidation I reached inside the bag and pulled out a bundle of money wrapped with a rubber band.

Ralph had a good life as a doctor and I have to say in my adult years I had enjoyed the comforts of being middle class. But this... I flipped the edges of the money with my fingers and whistled. Where did Leesa get all that money? This was a girl who couldn't keep a job for more than a few months.

My instincts were tingling. Something wasn't right the moment Leesa showed up on my doorstep. I'd barely had time to give Mary a thought today, but the creepiness of my former friend's body and now my daughter's disappearing act made me nervous.

I stuffed the bundle of bills back into the diaper bag. If I knew my daughter, she would be back for her stash. I prayed if she stole the money, that someone wouldn't be right behind her. Even more importantly, I prayed they hadn't caught up with her.

God, what's happening? My whole world had turned upside down in less than twenty-four hours. So much for the quiet, retired life.

8

The inquiring-minds-want-to-know twins eyed me as I entered the church vestibule. Annie Mae and Willie Mae Brown had been staples at Missionary Baptist Church for as long as I could remember. They also ran the usher board, pastor's aid board, missionary board and any other board where they could stick their noses.

I could tell they were not too happy with me since I just walked through the doors without my white dress and orthopedic white shoes. Standard usher uniform. With thirty minutes to get ready, I prayed protection over Leesa (from me), then I stuffed the diaper bag with the suspicious contents in the back of my closet. In the process, an old favorite brushed against my face beckoning me to pull it off the hanger. Despite all that happened in the previous twenty-four hours, I was plum pleased I could fit my hips into my pale pink suit.

It's amazing I still owned the suit, since so many other clothing treasures had long since been passed on to Goodwill or the Salvation Army. My body lost the battle with keeping up with a reputable dress size once I stopped being able to squeeze into a size eighteen. That was a sad day.

With the way my day had gone so far, it would be best to pass by the twins before they commented on missing my Sunday morning duty.

Annie Mae dashed over to me, blocking my path. She cooed at Tyric, but her one good eye checked out my attire. "Ooooh, look at the pretty baby."

"Whose baby, Eugeena?" Annie Mae's identical twin Willie Mae, ambushed me on the other side. The only way I could tell the two apart, besides Annie Mae's wandering eye, was Willie Mae's facial features. Her face always seemed rounder and softer than her sister's. Even her skin had an angelic glow. What a farce.

Anyone who spent time around the twins would have found out that behind Willie Mae's sweet face was the worst gossip. The oldest twin, by a minute, could instigate a situation into existence with as much time as it took for her to come into the world before her twin.

It paid to be careful. So, I proceeded to act speechless. "Well I... uh."

"Eugeena, why would you keep a new grandbaby from us?"

"Yeah? What's going on?"

Poor little Kisha peered up from behind me at the two woman. Her eyes were huge. With both sisters closing in on me, I started to feel my body perspire. I was not messing up my suit.

"Good morning, ladies. Y'all sure looking mighty fine this morning."

Annie Mae and Willie Mae spun around. Both women looked like they'd been hit.

I knew the affect Amos Jones had on me. In some ways, I'm glad he came to my rescue, but would I have to return the favor? These women could easily send Amos back into hiding in his backyard or fishing on Sunday.

Too late. The twins went into action. Each tried to push a church bulletin into Amos' hand. He was an eligible bachelor and if young women had it bad, women our age certainly had some slim pickings from the male population.

I wasn't looking myself. God had sent me enough trouble, and I wasn't trying to look for more.

I sped ahead of Amos down the aisle. We came to church together, but I didn't have time for wagging tongues. I had more serious matters to be worried about.

We arrived a little late, so I had to make my way down near the front of the already filled pews. I forgot it was the Sunday to honor the graduates, so more occupants were in the sanctuary than usual.

Good thing I had on my comfy shoes. Tyric was getting a little tiresome to hold and I had to create an alternative diaper bag on the fly. That meant I stuffed diapers and bottles in my own bag which already held a drugstore supply. I'm sure the bulging bag didn't label me a fashion diva. I wasn't trying to compete with the First Lady or the elite section of the church, but unfortunately that's where I had to sit this morning.

One head after the other turned to watch as I squeezed my way into the pew. Even when the Missionary Baptist Gospel Choir started singing many people still broke their necks to look in my direction. My cheekbones burned from smiling so hard. These are the benefits of attending a small church. Everybody wanted to be in your business.

Then it hit me. By now most of the congregation probably heard about Mary's demise. Years ago, Mary and I sat on the same pew, taking turns pinching each other's children when they got out of order. Those days were precious and now gone forever. My stubbornness caused me to lose more than I imagined.

It really did get bad between us, with some folks in the church choosing sides.

Sometimes it paid to leave other folks out of your business. Didn't Paul say somewhere to talk to that person and work it out? I should've paid better attention to that bible lesson. Maybe Mary wouldn't have left the church.

"Hello, Miss Eugeena."

Too busy trying to get Kisha and myself seated I didn't notice Tamara on the pew beside us. "Hey honey. It's so good to see you visiting Missionary." I'd sent out the invitation to her a few times. That Carmen too. It was hard to get young people in church sometime. Missionary Baptist wasn't the most innovative or contemporary, but we loved to praise the Lord.

"Are these your grandchildren?" Tamara had her eyes on Kisha and then swung them to Tyric who amazingly still slept like a log. "Can I hold him?"

"Well …" I'd just met my own grandson last night. I'm not sure how he would react to a stranger. "Sure, why not." I passed Tyric's sleeping body over to Tamara. She looked at him adoringly and then brushed her hands against his face.

I cringed thinking the baby would start screeching. If he did, I would have to grab all our stuff and march right back up the aisle, past the twins, and to the nursery.

Like a trooper, Tyric slept on.

Tamara will make a good mama someday.

The choir picked up the pace of the song with some down home clapping.

Praise the Lord. Everybody ought to praise the Lord.

I looked down at the sweet little one beside me. Kisha clapped her tiny hands off beat to the song and sang, "Praise the Low. Praise the Low."

I tapped Kisha's shoulder. "It's Lord."

Precious thing smiled and kept right on clapping, "Praise the Low."

Don't know if you call it déjà-vu, but I recalled a similar memory with Leesa.

Sitting on the other side of Kisha, Amos bopped his head from side to side. I was surprised he'd chosen to sit on the same pew as us. This was the first time in awhile I'd seen him without a hat. He had a perfectly round bald head, no dents or lumps.

Coming to church this morning had to be difficult for him. He used to come faithfully before his wife died, pushing her down the aisle in a wheelchair during the latter part of her illness.

Deacon Moses shuffled to and then kneeled at the altar. Fifteen minutes later, Kisha wiggled beside me. I thought about pinching her, but then it crossed my mind that I wanted to pinch the deacon. I believed Deacon Moses should have long been finished with that prayer. Really, the man repeated the same request for forgiveness three times. He obviously had a bad week, but did we all need to hear about it.

Oh Lord Jesus, forgive me.

Actually every time the deacon mentioned forgiveness, all I could think about was poor Mary. Her blank eyes stared at me from my memory of finding her ... Was it only yesterday? It felt like a week ago. Now Mary would never know how sorry I was for my stubborn refusal to see the truth.

Tears flooded my eyes and sorrow enveloped my soul.

A flash of gold caught my eyes from the left. It was the offering plate on the move down the pew. At the end of both pews, one of twins was positioned. I felt a little safe being in the middle, but their stares still bothered me.

Tamara passed Tyric back to me. I looked down at his face, really a stranger to me, but he'd taken to me and me to him. I turned to tell Tamara thank you, but she had already reached the end of the pew. She sprinted toward the back. Either she had a bathroom run or was upset about something.

I pulled dollar bills out the side of my pocket book. The pile of money on the offering plate reminded me of what was hidden in my closet back home. I prayed that girl hadn't robbed a bank or worse. What was really crazy? Why did she leave the money? When I realized Leesa had left Kisha's booster seat and Tyric's carrier in my car I'd almost lost it. What was the girl up to?

I laid my thoughts aside as Pastor Jones stood up. The big man hadn't said a single word, but his ebony forehead glistened under the chandelier that hung above the pulpit. This sermon must be a doozy.

"Church, what do you do when trouble comes? That's my message this morning."

My ears pricked up. Trouble had been chasing me for the past twenty-four hours. I wanted God to pull me out the hot grease before I got burned to a crisp.

"From the book of Job, we are familiar with the calamities that hit Job. One by one, his world was rocked. But ole' Job, he kept his faith in the Lord. If you remember from the passage, his friends came by with their own opinions. Not much help."

No, they weren't. I moved Tyric to my other arm. It's been awhile since I held a child. This child had a heavy head. I always thought it was peculiar the way young mamas carried their child in them carriers. I should've brought the carrier in with me. I just about had no feeling in my arm.

"Church, you can't listen to folks around you. You have to keep your ears tuned into God. We don't know what his plans are for us, but he knows best."

Something stirred inside me as Pastor Jones continued. Job was really disappointed in his friends. Instead of being there for him after he had lost it all, the know-it-alls just picked the poor man apart.

I had a friend who was a good person and meant well. Due to my own self-righteousness, I turned my back on her. Now she was gone. Forever.

My world had shifted. I'm glad God was in control because the feeling in the pit of my stomach told me, *Sistah, you ain't seen nothing yet.*

9

I hated to say I should have seen the ambush coming, but I didn't. Between Pastor Jones' sermon, my loss of a dear friend and a MIA daughter, I forgot to prepare myself.

Holding Mr. Amos' hand, Kisha had skipped ahead of me. The sight warmed my heart. As I recalled, Amos had grandkids of his own, but they lived somewhere on the west coast. I'm not even sure if I'd seen any of his kids since his wife died.

Before I reached the vestibule to shake the pastor's hand, the twins cornered me.

"It's a sad thing." Annie Mae shook her head.

This puzzled me, "What's sad?"

"You know?"

I turned towards Willie Mae. She had a lopsided smile on her face. I wish I knew where this conversation was headed. Those two old biddies were dropping hints like we were in the twilight zone or something.

Other members pushed past us, some giving us ugly looks. It wasn't my fault the twins decided to interrogate me in the middle of the church aisle.

Willie Mae leaned down and cupped her mouth, whispering. "Mary. It's a shame about her death."

"Yeah, we heard you found her." Annie Mae's breath floated across my nostrils, a mixture of coffee and tobacco. I didn't dare inhale again until she moved out my line of breathing. Annie Mae posed as the saint of all saints, but she couldn't lay down her stronghold with chewing tobacco.

I took two steps backward since Annie Mae insisted on breathing toxic fumes over me. "Yes. Look I'm still ... well, I can't talk right now."

Willie Mae pulled her arm down in front of me like a stop sign on a bus. Why wouldn't these two leave me be and let me pass?

"Honey, you okay? Maybe you should sit down. This must be a shock to you seeing how you two used to be such good friends."

I didn't want to and wouldn't sit down. "I'm fine. Yes, I'm going to miss her."

"You two never did make up. Oh, but I guess that would've been hard considering Mary had a breakdown and everything." Willie Mae smiled, but her words sliced through the air like a Ninja going in for the kill.

That was her mistake. Mary and I weren't close for the past five years, but she was a godly person. A bigger woman than I ever could be. I wouldn't stand for her name to be smeared even before her body was laid in her final resting place.

"Now you two listen here. If I'm not mistaken both of y'all have been through some tough times." I pointed at each sister, looking them both in the eyes. Annie Mae, her one good eye.

"Mary lost her family and she had a right to grieve. She wasn't crazy and I won't hear anything like that come from either of you again."

Sucking in her breath, Willie Mae touched her chest. "Oh now Eugeena, Annie Mae and I loved Mary as much as you. We know she had it hard. Calm down."

"Yeah, we were really concerned about you finding her body. The cops must have really wanted to talk to you."

Oh my Lord!

If I wasn't still standing in the church sanctuary, I would've ... well. I was scared of my thoughts. God said pour good on your enemies head. I needed to walk away now before applying that principle slipped my mind. "Have a blessed afternoon, ladies."

Before I took two steps, Willie Mae's voice rang out. "You know the cops been asking questions. We're church folks and we can't cover up the truth."

Annie Mae agreed, "No sister, that wouldn't be right in the eyes of God."

I didn't bother to turn around. I couldn't. I would've seen the same self-righteous smirk on those two women I had seen so many times before. Plus, I was holding my new grandbaby. No time for foolishness. I had enough of that to deal with when I returned home.

Besides I had nothing to hide from the police. So I got angry with an old friend, fussed her out in the church parking lot and then ignored her existence for months. Months turned to years of indifference. I had plenty of opportunities to reconcile our friendship. It became easier to leave the past alone as time went by.

Finally, I reached the pastor. Pastor George Jones was probably my favorite pastor ever. His father, Rev. Tennessee Jones, the one who co-founded this church and who remained the pastor most of the thirty-some years I attended had gone on to glory late last year. His son was about the age of my oldest son and appeared to be holding his own. This couldn't be an easy assignment for a man in his late-thirties. Most of the congregation knew him when he'd sported nothing but a diaper.

"Sister Patterson, how are you and who's this cute little fellow?" Pastor Jones touched Tyric's little hand. Now awake, Tyric peered up at the preacher, looking puzzled by the new face.

"My... my grandchild." I croaked. I wanted to tell the pastor I could give ole' Job some competition about having the worst day of your life, but that wasn't entirely true. Just felt that way. My soul was troubled and even now more so thanks to Willie Mae and Annie Mae. Instead I said, "Pastor Jones, your sermon this morning was something else."

"I'm glad you liked it, Sister. I am terribly sorry to hear about Sister Fleming's passing. That's an awful way to leave this world. I know God has her in his arms."

"Oh, I don't doubt that. Mary was a dear soul."

"Well, I spoke to Mary's eldest sister this morning before service. It looks like the funeral will be on Thursday. She did have a request. Sister Patterson, would you be willing to say a few words on behalf of the church?"

Me?

I remembered Mary's sister, Natalie. Hadn't seen her in years. From what I remember, both sisters weren't that close. Surely, she would know I was not the person who needed to be speaking at her sister's funeral.

I stared at Pastor Jones. He was pastoring at another church during the time Mary and I had our falling out. Maybe he doesn't know about the blow up between us. There were few members who didn't know. I could imagine the smirks on the twins' faces from the front row on Thursday. Could I even stand beside Mary's casket and call myself having words to say? The entire scenario seemed a tiny bit awkward.

"Pastor, I don't know if I'm the right person to speak at her funeral."

"I know it will be a hard time for you. But please consider. I think you would be the perfect person."

"Thank you, Pastor. I appreciate you asking me."

After I stepped outside, it took me a few moments to get adjusted to the early afternoon sun. I used my free hand to wipe some moisture from my eyes. I couldn't blame it on my bifocals. Through my rapid blinking, I saw the parking lot was pretty empty except for a few cars. I appreciated not having anyone see how torn up I really felt.

Amos smiled when he saw me, but his face changed to concern. "Everything alright?"

"I'm fine. Thanks for looking out for Kisha."

"My pleasure."

I buckled Tyric in the car seat and then made sure little Kisha was fastened into her booster seat. I'm happy they have all these safety measures these days. I shudder to think of all the ways my own children traveled in the car.

I still couldn't believe the audacity of my daughter. Couldn't she have asked me instead of assuming I would keep her kids while she was Lord knows where?

Amos drove up beside me in his truck. We came in separate vehicles, but he'd followed me over to the church. "You sure you are doing okay, Eugeena?"

He really was a sweet man. "I'm fine, Amos. I hope you enjoyed service this morning."

"Sure did. I will follow y'all to make sure you get home safe."

Amos seemed determined to act as my guardian angel. I can't say I was complaining. After all, I was the one whining to God about being lonely. Have to be careful what you pray for sometimes.

In about ten minutes, I pulled into the driveway of my house. There were still no signs of Leesa's Altima anywhere. It was the car her dad gave her, probably the last gift she'd received from her dad before he passed. I gave her credit for at least keeping up with the car. It was paid in full and there wasn't a need for her not to maintain it.

As I unbuckled Tyric, I heard raised voices in the distance. Sounded like a man and a woman. Not wanting to be nosy, I peered through the back window of the car. Across the street, Tamara was waving her hands in a man's face. Come to think about it, Tamara never did return to her seat after the offering. She must have left the church and went home.

I could only see the man from the backside, but I assumed he must be her husband.

With Kisha dawdling behind me and Tyric in my arms, I glanced back over at the couple. The man proceeded to get in the red sports car, and backed out the driveway. He took off down the street, burning rubber in the process. Poor Tamara stood with her arms folded. If I didn't have the children with me, I would've walked over to her. Married life was hard. I should know. As much misery as it brought me I missed Ralph.

Tyric started wailing. Must have meant it was time to eat. I decided to try to reach out to Tamara later.

We had only been in the house all of fifteen minutes when the doorbell rang.

Now who could that be?

Maybe Tamara came over to vent.

Still holding Tyric, who seemed to have become a member of my body, I peeked through the door's peephole. My visitor's eyes were hidden behind dark shades, but I could tell from her stance it was a very official visit.

10

When I opened the door, I almost expected Detective Wilkes to pull out handcuffs and start spouting my Miranda rights. But of course that would be silly. I didn't do anything. Still, her showing up at my house a second time in two days couldn't be good.

I'm sure by now she'd talked to a lot of people and heard all kinds of stories. Especially if Willie Mae or Annie Mae had a chance to bend the detective's ear for a minute or two. Those drama-starting queens.

"Mrs. Patterson, I'm sorry to catch you after church. Do you have a few minutes?"

"Sure, why don't you come in? I do need to get these children something to eat if you don't mind."

"Not at all. Take your time." Detective Wilkes grinned at Kisha and reached her hand out to touch her head. "Hey cutie."

Kisha shrank back from the detective. Her caramel skin proceeded to radiate a reddish glow followed by an ear-piercing scream. Little Tyric decided to join in with his own squall.

"Good heavens, Kisha. Is that called for?"

Two hysterical kids were going to work my nerves in the worst way possible. I could see the headline now, "Grandmother Loses it in Front of Cop." I wanted Leesa to pick up her children, not Child Protective Services.

After thirty minutes, I had the two howlers fed and settled down for naps. Maybe I would be allowed an afternoon siesta. Pulling the covers over my head for awhile would be what Eugeena ordered for herself.

My prescription for rest would come later. I joined the detective in the living room where she had made herself at home. "Sorry, about all the commotion, Detective Wilkes."

"Not a problem. You have a nice home, Mrs. Patterson."

"Thank you." I had a feeling I might have a lot of explaining to do. "You said you had some questions for me."

The detective flipped some pages in her notepad. "Tell me a little about your relationship with Mary Fleming. How long were you friends?"

"Why is that important?"

"Sounds like you might have known her the best. Would you say she had any enemies?"

Enemies. God has some sense of humor. Mary and I had been the best of friends. We lived down the street from each other, our children played together, our husbands went fishing and we even taught at the same junior high school for years. She taught English and me, social studies. We probably spent more time in each other's classrooms sharing our woes than with other teachers in our own departments.

Then it all changed.

Would I classify myself as Mary's enemy?

I remember it like yesterday. Mary came over just as nice as she could. An aroma wafted from the cloth-covered object in her hands. I let my nose inhale one of my favorite scents. I was known as the cake and cookie baker, while Mary was the one known for her pies.

Now that day the apple pie would've been a nice offer, because it sure smelled heavenly, but the next words out of Mary's mouth, made me want to smash that golden crust creation in her face. Never did get a slice of that pie.

I gulped and looked at Detective Wilkes' face. "No, I couldn't imagine anyone not liking Mary. She stuck close to herself in later years, but mainly out of grief."

"I understand she had some tragedy."

"Yes, about five years ago, she lost her husband and her only daughter in a car accident. She's been withdrawn since then."

"I understand there was some animosity between you two."

Here we go. "Yes, our friendship suffered a setback over an incident. At the time I was too pig-headed to see that Mary was telling the truth. By then it was too late."

"Want to share the details?"

Do I have a choice?

"Our girls were good friends back then. My daughter Leesa went over to the Flemings' for a slumber party. Sometime during the night, Mary's daughter, Jennifer, Leesa and some other girls got into Mary's jewelry."

A memory of Mary's face. The hurt. My emotions at the moment. It all came back.

"Mrs. Patterson?"

"Oh, I'm sorry. One of the pieces of jewelry went missing. It was an heirloom passed down in Mary's family from I don't know ... late 1800s. It was valuable and very precious to Mary."

"Did she say why she kept it in the jewelry box?"

"I have no idea. I've always asked myself that question. She might have mentioned she wore it for special occasions. Anyhow, she told me her daughter thought Leesa took the ring. I asked Leesa about it, she said she did wear it for awhile, but she took it off and placed it back in the jewelry box."

"It really seems so silly now, but it just got out of hand. Mary was talking to people and I vented to people that Mary was slandering my daughter's name calling her a thief and..."

"Mrs. Patterson, I looked up some information. Do you know where I can find your daughter?"

The air conditioner vent was on the other side of the room, but a chill ran down my arm. "Why? I mean I thought you were here to ask me about Mary?"

Detective Wilkes cleared her throat. "Your daughter, when she was younger, she did have a problem with taking things. Right?"

Not again. No, no, no, I knew my silence answered the detective's question. But what could I say. Not too long after the incident at the Fleming's, Leesa did get caught shoplifting among other things.

All that time I defended her, she made me eat every last righteous word I'd foamed at the mouth about my child.

"Mrs. Patterson, if you can tell me how to get in touch with Leesa, I really need to talk to her."

I narrowed my eyes. Leesa was still my child, my baby. I don't know what she'd gotten into, but this detective wouldn't be talking to her at least not without a lawyer. I hoped it didn't come down to that. But I had to expect the worst.

Leesa's surprises were not for the faint of heart.

"Detective, I can't tell you where my daughter is right now, but I would like to know why you came over here asking for her?"

The woman stood. "It would be best for her if she came in. Right now, she's a person of interest to me."

I jumped up. "For what? Are you trying to say you suspect my daughter of something?"

Lord knows what it could be. I knew I might have the evidence upstairs in my closet.

"Mrs. Patterson, calm down. We have a witness who saw a woman, a young woman leaving Mary's house late last Friday night. I understand your daughter drives a late model Nissan Altima, aqua blue?"

"Yes, but it couldn't have been Leesa. She just came here last night..." I shut my mouth realizing my error a tad bit too late.

The detective's jaw hardened. She looked toward my staircase and then back at me. I almost thought she was going to take off and head upstairs. The detective wouldn't find

Leesa. I watched enough television cop shows to know she needed a search warrant to step her foot anywhere else in my house and I wasn't about to give her permission. I certainly didn't need her to find the money in the diaper bag.

"Mrs. Patterson, your daughter could've been the last person who saw Mary alive. I will be looking to see her at the station soon. You enjoy the rest of your Sunday afternoon."

I closed the door behind the detective. What had Leesa done this time and why would she visit Mary? If she did go over to Mary's, did she see something?

Out of all the scenarios I had conjured up in my mind, I could not and would not fathom my daughter being a murder suspect. If anything, she was probably one scared young woman and I had to find her.

11

The past forty-eight hours had not been kind to my central nervous system. I didn't like the term black sheep, but Leesa had pressed my buttons enough for me to call her my "special" child. This wasn't the first time Leesa had gone missing; it had just been awhile since she tried that stunt. I hoped that this missing-in-action was only about an opportunity to get away and clear her head. But of what? What set the child off?

After Mary accused her of stealing, Leesa started disappearing for hours and a few times, for days. Ralph and I aged during Leesa's moments of rebellion as well as her despair over losing her friend in the car accident. The day Leesa came to me in pain; little did I know the emergency room visit would produce the birth of my third grandchild.

My daughter took surprises to a whole other level. Her weight concealed any signs of life. To this day, I still don't know if she knew she was pregnant.

I looked over on the couch where my granddaughter lie fast asleep. Kisha wanted to stay up to see some show. I caved. Did the same thing when the twins came over too. I wouldn't let my children stay up past nine o'clock. Benefits of being a grandchild, I guess.

I picked up Kisha and carried her to the room that belonged to her mother. Her younger brother had long been put to bed. Tyric slept peacefully with pillows surrounding him.

As I laid Kisha next to her brother, her eyelids opened half way. "Mama. Where's mama?"

I wish I knew, honey. "Don't worry. Your mama will be back soon."

I bent down to kiss her forehead. This was such a sweet age. I wasn't sure when Leesa lost her sweetness. It might have been in middle school. Someone snatched up my sweet girl and replaced her with some attitude-popping-girl-woman. It didn't help that Leesa had developed a voluptuous figure, thanks to my side of the family. She became a cute girl who craved attention from all the wrong people.

The collisions between father and daughter were memorable to put it nicely. Ralph would demand Leesa's obedience and she would do the exact opposite. You would've thought after Jennifer Fleming and her dad's death in the car accident, it would've sobered the two up. It didn't.

Leesa didn't back down from her rebellious spirit until Ralph's first heart attack. Not too long after her father died, Leesa gradually drifted away. Usually some new boyfriend held her attention until they broke up and she needed money.

Little Tyric moved in his sleep, placing his thumb in his mouth. This child I didn't even know about until two days before.

Now who is your daddy?

I could ask myself how and why, but those questions could wait. I needed Leesa to show up soon. No matter what she did or how she felt about me, I was her mother and she needed me.

The phone rang in the distance. I moved out the door as fast as I could and closed it slightly behind me. I raced inside the bedroom and grabbed the phone.

"Leesa?"

"Eugeena? No, it's me, Louise. Is everything alright?"

I contained my groan. "Hey Louise, what can I do for you?"

"Well, I don't know about you, but I'm just nervous. Last night I didn't sleep and it doesn't look like I'm going to get any shut-eye tonight. Is this a bad time?"

You have no idea, woman.

Deflated, I needed to hear from my daughter, not woes from a little old lady.

Okay, I know that's not nice, Lord.

Louise was dear to me. We did just have a murder down the street. If the detective hadn't come by asking about my daughter, who happened to be a person of interest, maybe I would be feeling more like Louise now. I was in a defenseless situation myself, not that young, at least sixty pounds overweight and I had two small children in the house.

"Louise, honey, just make sure you check all your doors. You have been using the AC, right? Do not keep the windows open. We talked about plenty of safety precautions at the first neighborhood meeting."

"Believe me. Everything is shut tight. But you know, Eugeena, that's what's bothering me. Did you know the police said there wasn't a break-in over at Mary's?"

"Are you sure?"

I didn't want to get into how Louise knew, but this little tidbit worried me. If it wasn't a break-in that meant Mary invited her "killer" inside. Being a cautious person, Mary would have only allowed a person she knew well into her home.

I needed to get off the phone and keep the line open. "Louise, I'm tired. It's been a long day. How about me and you get together soon and brainstorm? We need to talk about the agenda for next neighborhood meeting."

"We will have a lot to talk about. You have a good evening, Eugeena."

I hung up the phone. I wasn't really interested in planning the next meeting, but I needed to give my busybody neighbor something else to do.

Who else would Mary invite inside her home besides Leesa? I wasn't all that convinced it was Leesa because none of my children had spoken to or been in contact with Mary in years.

I grabbed a notebook from the desk and started jotting down neighbors' names. I really didn't know everyone in the neighborhood like I used to, but someone reported seeing Leesa. Leesa rarely came around so it had to be a neighbor who had lived in Sugar Creek for some time.

Wayne. Leesa had a crush on him when she was a little girl. At one time, Wayne really was a good boy. All-star football player, he and my middle child Cedric were buddies. Cedric attended college, and Wayne enlisted in the army. I had prayed and twisted my hands with his mama as he served in Desert Storm. When he came back, the Wayne we once knew was replaced by a moody man, prone to consuming too much alcohol. No matter what he did or how hard his mama prayed and begged, he stayed in trouble. One time he went too far.

I still wasn't clear about the charges against Wayne, but he remained in jail for at least three years. Poor Agnes died while he served his time. I really should be more motherly instead of being so ornery towards the boy. I just didn't trust him. Mainly because I expected a man to dress and act like a man. Wayne did neither. I can't accuse him of being a killer, but he was a trained soldier.

Then, there was Carmen. Only been here less than a year. I'm sure she didn't know Leesa. Maybe it was mistaken identity. Carmen was much taller than Leesa, but they shared a similar complexion. Other than seeing her jog by the house, coming and going in her car, I didn't know much about her. She drove a Toyota Camry, an earlier model than the one I drove. Carmen wouldn't need to use a car since she could easily walk to Mary's home. Did they even know each other?

Who else? Tamara. She wasn't sure what the woman did for a living. Tamara seemed to live the life of a desperate housewife. Always home and not very happy.

I jotted down a few more names, but couldn't see where anyone had a motive. I put my pen down. This list was sounding more like a gossip column. All this speculating was going nowhere. Just reminded me of how well I had isolated myself and gotten caught up in the routine of getting up in the morning, teaching my class periods and returning home in the evenings to grade papers and stuff my face.

Since Ralph's death, I hadn't taken the time to meet new neighbors or reconnect with older ones other than Louise and now Amos. It used to not be like this. Neighbors being such strangers. Years ago, when the children were younger we had block parties. The women supplied the side dishes and the men would cook meat on their grills. Right out there in the street.

A block party! Now that's an idea I could discuss with Louise to propose for the next meeting.

How else would we be able to keep the neighborhood safe, if we didn't try to get to know each other? Old retired bird like me had plenty of time on her hands to set things right.

Set things right, Eugeena.

Who was I fooling? I caused chaos. I lost a friend a long time ago and my daughter barely spoke to me unless she had to.

I looked over at the closet. Leesa would come back. Why else would she leave that bundle of cash? Unless she planned to be gone a long time. Or was that it? She left the cash for me to take care of her kids. That didn't ease my mind about where it came from.

Overwhelmed with my thoughts, it was time to lay my burdens down. I kneeled by my bed. Tears rolled down the side of my face. "Lord, I need you right now. Why do the ones we love cause us the most pain? I guess you know more so than anybody knows about that type of pain, Lord. Please bring Leesa back to me. I trust you will keep her safe. And my friend, my dear friend Mary. Lord, help me find justice for her. I don't understand any of what's happened the past few days, but I know you will make everything alright. Amen."

One thing I was confident of, I would never believe my child committed murder.

12

The pinkish glow peeking through my bedroom window signaled my appointed time had come. God had nudged me awake to see another morning. With all that had happened I was grateful. I closed my eyes and opened my heart to hear the still small voice. I can't say it was so much an audible voice, but more of a knowing deep in my spirit. The Lord was moving and I needed to get up.

First thing on my agenda was to gather some help. I couldn't do anything by myself and I was determined to track down Leesa. She had her places to hide and there were people I could nudge to tell me what they knew. I headed downstairs, cautious not to wake the children, but my weight caused the stairs to creak anyway. It was crucial for me to get a few things done before the children rose.

In the kitchen, Porgy lifted his head when I entered. I know he wanted to be on my bed, but I wasn't quite ready for that part of owning a dog. It was enough to have him in the house at all. Before I went to bed last night we came to an agreement or at least I did. His area would be in a corner of the kitchen. He followed me around with his tail wagging, so I imagined he had a decent night's sleep. Better than me.

I dreamed about Leesa and the bag of money. She was dressed up with a mask like the girls in that Queen Latifah movie I saw years ago. *Dreaming of your child robbing a bank. Eugeena, what kind of mother are you?* It wasn't like it was big bag of money. Had to be at least a thousand dollars though.

I started boiling the water for my morning green tea. With this lifestyle change sometimes I didn't recognize my own kitchen and its contents. Speaking of lifestyle changes, one person I needed to connect with was the main person who had been nagging me all these years to get my eating habits under control. Aunt Cora. Strangely, I didn't think of her as much of an aunt since she was two years older. Cora was the sister I never had and a true woman of God.

I dialed the number that I should've dialed the moment Leesa arrived. If there was any female relative in the family Leesa was close to, Cora would be the number one candidate.

"Eugeena, girl why you calling so early this Monday morning? You supposed to be enjoying your retirement by sleeping in late."

I cackled. "I wish. And how you know it was me?"

"Caller ID, Sistah. You know you need to get with it. All the young'uns you taught, I know you should be more up-to-date on technology than that."

"You know I really don't want to know more than my brain can handle."

We laughed. "So, what's going on?" Cora's voice softened. "I saw the news last night when I came back in from church. Why didn't you call me by now about Mary? You in shock I imagine."

"Oh, Cora. I'm more than in shock. I have a pure dilemma on my hands. I can't explain it all right now, but I need you to help me figure out some things and lift up some prayers this morning."

"What's going on?"

I closed my eyes. "Leesa. She came by the other night. Left her children. You know she has two now."

"Oh."

"Oh. That's all you have to say. The girl just dropped the kids off and disappeared."

"She did. Lord, help that child. Did you even know about the baby?"

"No I didn't." Something struck me strange the way Cora asked me that question. "Did you know?"

A long sigh on the other side of the call answered my question. "I told her she needed to tell you. I could tell the time that girl walked in the door she was carrying more than just her weight."

My face felt as though I'd been slapped. "When was this… she always confides in you, Cora. I'm her mother."

"Wait now! Don't get upset. I was surprised by the first child too. Remember? Girl, if I could explain your child's logic, I would. To be honest she seemed a bit in denial about the whole thing. I had to ask her if she was on something."

No, no. That was the one good thing about Leesa. In all her troubles, she didn't touch drugs. Alcohol was another thing, but she stayed clear of the hard stuff. "You still didn't tell me the last time you saw her?"

"This was about a month ago, Eugeena. I was really surprised to see her. Have you thought to check her place out?"

"It's on my agenda. I'm going to ask the neighbor to watch the kids while I drive up to her apartment in Columbia. I've been calling the home and cell phone, but both appear to be out of service. I just hope she still has the apartment."

"Don't worry yourself. God has been looking out for that child since you had her. Wherever she is, you'll find her. I pray God's protection over you and her."

"We need all the prayers that we can get because when I get my hands on her…"

"Now, Eugeena, keep yourself under control. Find her and get her home. And please make sure you take care of yourself. You checked your sugar levels today, right? How's that glucose meter working for you?"

"Look at you. You a retired nurse and can't seem to stop checking up on somebody."

"I know you. You will be so caught up in finding Leesa; you will let your health slide. Your children need you in this world a little longer. Keep me updated. Don't wait so long to call next time."

That's what I needed. Some reinforcements. Now I needed to move to next on my list.

The babies would be up soon, both hungry. There was someone else who might appreciate breakfast this morning. I pulled down ingredients of the shelf to make cheese grits. Soon I had turkey bacon sizzling in my cast iron skillet.

An hour later, I had a three folks at my table. Kisha's eyes were glued to the small TV in the corner. Tyric sucked milk greedily from his bottle. Across from me, Amos shoveled grits off his plate into his mouth like he hadn't eaten for days.

"So you like the baked cheese grits?" I smiled.

"Oh yeah. This is good. I can't wait to try that fried chicken you promised me." Amos winked.

My cheeks grew warm. I know I wasn't trying to blush, but I was right about him being a fried chicken man. I would have to keep my promise, but first... "Amos, I need your help."

"Sure. What can I help you with?"

I wasn't so sure how much I should tell Amos, especially with young ears at the kitchen table. I peered over at Kisha who appeared to be trying to feed Porgy again. "Uh-uh Kisha, Porgy does not eat from the table." Goodness Mary had spoiled this dog something awful. He thought he was a little person or something.

I turned my attention back to Amos who was scraping his plate with the side of his fork. I must say I missed having a man around my table. One thing I did do right with Ralph was satisfy his appetite. He didn't go hungry or have to worry about not having a good meal. I'm sure my cooking didn't help him, but Ralph was a doctor and chose to eat what he liked.

It was rather nice to fix a healthy meal and see someone enjoy it. Instead of admiring the man, I needed to get his help.

"Amos, you were a cop, right?"

"Spent ten years as cop and twenty years as a homicide detective."

"You don't say. Well, I guess you've seen quite a bit in your years."

"I would say, nothing surprises me."

"People can do the strangest things. I'm still in shock about Mary."

"You know, if you hadn't went over there, no telling when someone would've found Mary's body."

"That's right, but I don't think that's going to help me. In fact I have a bit of a predicament with the detective conducting the investigation."

"Wilkes. She can be a tough cookie. Heard she was the best."

"I'm sure she is, but I'm really wondering about this witness?"

"Witness?" Amos frowned and cocked his eyebrow. "Well, what did this witness see?"

"Someone I know. There has to be some mistake."

"Mmm, well I can certainly inquire about the case for you."

"Would you? That would mean so much to me."

"I can't guarantee that Wilkes will run her mouth. These cases are pretty confidential from the public, but maybe someone will share some insight. I have a few fishing buddies in the department." Amos leaned forward in the chair, "Now you're not thinking about doing your own investigation?"

"Oh no. Well, not without your help of course." I smiled and this time I *know* I batted my eyelashes.

Amos responded, "I don't know, Eugeena."

"You know people are looking for me to have information being the head of this neighborhood watch."

"Yeah, but some things need to be left to the professionals."

"I know. But the ..." I glanced at Kisha. "The k-i-l-l-e-r had to be someone Mary knew. Could be somebody we all know. A birdie told me there was no sign of a break-in at Mary's place." I didn't want to let Amos know the birdie was Louise from next door, but then again he might have already known.

Amos rubbed his chin. "That is odd. If they didn't take anything, then they went in either with the sole purpose to hurt Mary or something went wrong, maybe an argument. Still, you know the person who entered Mary's house could have driven into the neighborhood."

That's true and not what I wanted to hear, since it only pointed more towards Leesa who didn't live here anymore. "Amos, I don't know if you know this since you haven't been in the neighborhood long, but Mary and I were good friends at one time. I just don't want her ..." I had to remember Kisha was probably listening though her eyes were turned toward the TV. "I don't want her demise to go without justice. She suffered a lot these last years. With her tragedies, she still did good for other people."

"I understand. But just keep in mind, you need to be careful. If it is someone in the neighborhood, that leaves you vulnerable. It probably won't hurt to get a better feel for who was where last Friday night."

What Amos didn't know was the first person on my mind to find out their whereabouts was my own flesh and blood. I pondered whether or not I should tell Amos about my daughter's predicament.

"Something else bothering you, Eugeena?"

My, my. It was almost scary the way Amos seemed to be reading my mind. "Well, I've been trying to decide if I should tell you. I have a feeling I might need your help. You see that witness reported seeing my daughter at Mary's house Friday night. I know that can't be."

Amos let out a long whistle. "Well, surely she can explain. Have her go down to the police and give her statement."

"I would." I looked away from Amos. "If I could find her."

"What do you mean?"

"Remember when she came with her children. I'm sure you noticed Sunday morning, she was gone. Amos, I need to find her and I need you to do me a favor?"

"Anything."

Amos Jones would never know how grateful I was to hear those words. Sometimes people have to be careful when they agree to any favor though. I hoped after the fact, Amos would still want to be my neighbor.

13

I still wasn't sure this was the right thing to do. But it was too late to turn back now. Time was of the essence here. I walked up to Amos' front porch and rapped my knuckles on the oak door. Amos opened the door, sporting a Kangol hat, a golf shirt and khakis. He looked more like he was going to the golf course versus a wild goose chase. Amos shook his head. "Are you ready?"

"Yes, let's go and thank you so much for doing this." With some trepidation, I had asked Amos to help me track down Leesa. He suggested the first logical place was to head to her apartment. For the next hour we traveled I-26 towards Columbia. I could tell Amos had set the cruise control because he drove the Caddy with ease. He drove the truck more than the Cadillac, which I guess used to be his wife's car. I felt a bit odd sitting in the passenger seat. Mrs. Amos Jones' perfume still lingered inside the car. Wasn't a brand I would have chosen. Not that it mattered.

Amos interrupted my thoughts. "So you didn't know about the baby until she showed up, huh?"

"We don't have the best mother-daughter relationship. I tried all I could with her."

"Well, don't feel bad, Eugeena. At least your children live close to you and when she really needed you, she came home."

"I guess you are right. Don't you have two daughters?"

Amos' jaw tightened. "Yeah. One is in California and the other in Seattle. We don't keep in touch much since Aubrey passed. I have three grandkids."

I felt really awful for Amos. Father's Day was coming up in about two weeks. Maybe his girls would touch base with him. "I'm sorry. It can be hard when the children get older. You get so caught up with them growing up and then when they are on their own, they live their own lives."

After Ralph died, I didn't dare want any of my children to think me insufficient to care for myself. Truth of the matter, I almost didn't tell any of them about my diabetes diagnosis. So many things change as you get older.

I glanced up to see the exit sign. Soon enough we would arrive in front of the apartment complex where my daughter had lived for at least a year now. I helped her move into the apartment. Anytime she relocated for whatever reason, I was there to assist with packing her belongings. If I didn't come to help, she would throw her belongings in boxes any old kind of way. No newspaper, towels or anything to try to cushion her breakables. That child never did learn how to appreciate her things.

We finally arrived at the apartment complex, an aluminum-sided overnight building project. The row after row of boxed-shaped buildings didn't appear very appealing. At least the landscape had finally grown since I had been there last. Now snapdragons, red, purple and yellow lined the sidewalk.

"Amos, you can pull over there. Her apartment is in the Q section." I didn't see any signs of Leesa's car, but that didn't mean she hadn't been around.

Amos parked the car and then we sat. A curtain in the window right across from us shifted. It appeared Leesa's downstairs neighbor was keeping an eye on things. Was she looking for Leesa too?

Amos prodded me. "You want me to come up with you or will you be okay?"

Did he think I was going to choke her if I saw her? That thought occurred to me, but I really wanted to find her. "I will be fine." I stepped out into the blazing hot sun. The sidewalk reflected the sunlight back into my eyes. I placed my Terminator shades on today. My children hated them, but they fit rather nicely over my bifocals.

I grimaced when I rounded the corner. The apartments had the kind of stairwell that dared you to take it on. It wasn't like I didn't have stairs of my own to deal with it at home, but at least mine were carpeted and didn't seem as steep. Or quite so many. One foot after the other, my extra pounds mocked as I climbed. I knocked on the door labeled Q7. With no response, I increased the intensity of my banging.

Someone else's door creaked open below.

"Boy, didn't I tell you that girl wasn't there. Why you keep doing all that banging?"

Boy? I walked over to the railing and leaned over as far as I dared. "I'm not a boy, but I am this girl's mother. Have you seen her?"

"Oh my."

I heard shuffling and soon found a face glowering up at me. The woman appeared to be about my age or slightly older. She had a short white hair that from a distance looked liked lamb's wool.

"You're her mother. Well, I'm sho' glad to see you. That girl needs to get her some new friends."

I went towards the top of the staircase and began to descend. "Friends? Are you saying somebody else has been here looking for her?"

"Only that boyfriend of hers. At least I guess he is. He used to always be here, but then I got the impression she might have kicked him to the curb."

I'd reached the bottom of the steps. The woman must have been no taller than 4'11. With my 5'3 frame, I felt like I towered over her. "Are you Mrs. Hattie?"

"Yes, I am. How did you know my name?"

"Kisha has mentioned your name a few times."

"Oh, that's my girl. Just as sweet as she can be. I do watch her from time to time. But I haven't seen Leesa in a few days though. Usually when she works nights, I keep Kisha for her. Now, when she had the other baby, I told her I might have to charge extra. Babies can be fussy. Anyway, I hadn't heard from her, so I figured she'd found someone else to babysit. Looks like she got you."

No, she didn't. I loved my grandkids, but I'd raised three kids already. Besides that, where was the father? Was this young man possibly related to Tyric? "Do you by any chance know where I can find this man?"

Hattie scrunched her face. The woman looked like she was in pain. "I don't know."

Now I felt stupid asking my next question, but since my child had failed to keep me in the loop. "Do you remember his name? I really am concerned. I haven't seen Leesa in a few days."

"All I can remember is she called him Chris. I only knew that because they liked to argue. Outside my window and my door."

"I'm sorry to hear that. Do you know what type of car he drove?"

Mrs. Hattie narrowed her eyes. "You sure ask a lot of questions. Like some cop. Anyhow, he drove a black pick-up truck most of the time I saw him. Don't ask me what kind."

"That's okay. You've been very helpful to me, Mrs. Hattie." We had walked outside the walkway. From where I stood, I could see Amos.

"Is that your husband?"

"Oh no. My husband passed years ago. That's a neighbor. I needed some help driving today."

"Mmmmm. Well, I do hope you find her. These young people these days, I would not want to be in their shoes. Your daughter seemed to be decent. Really quiet until that boy-friend of hers came by. I always thought she should lose him."

"Thank you. You've been pretty helpful." I marched back to Amos, probably with Hattie's eyes glued to my back. Once inside the car, I let out a loud sigh.

"I saw you talking to the neighbor. Any clues?"

"No, but her neighbor mentioned a man, I guess Leesa's boyfriend has been looking for her." As much as I didn't want to speculate, I couldn't help it. Was it possible this young man may be the cause of Leesa's disappearance? "I really don't know where to start next. Any ideas?"

"If you want my advice, you are going to have to consider getting some more help. It has been over twenty-four hours."

I looked over at Amos. "You mean report her missing. I can't do that. Detective Wilkes already wants to talk to her as a person of interest in a murder. Suppose they think she's on the run."

"Wouldn't you rather she be found safe?"

"Of course, I would."

"I promise. I will do whatever I can do to help, but if you think she might be in danger, we need to find her ASAP."

Murder. Missing persons. Danger. Why did my first week of retirement resemble an episode from *Law and Order?* I prayed we never made it to the part where I would see my child on trial for murder.

14

In my heart, I knew Amos was right. The relationship I once had with my little girl had become estranged. No matter that I carried her for nine month during the part of my life, where I should have been long finished with babies. Or that I received the brunt of criticism for her actions. I'm sure people thought I'd lost my parenting skills when it came to her. You just never know how a child is going to turn out. Despite our conflicts, Leesa was my daughter and I wanted her safe.

I walked into the police department, and waited patiently for a good five minutes, thinking the officer behind the desk would acknowledge my presence. When I realized the person on the other end of her conversation was definitely not an emergency, but more like a gabbing girlfriend, I rapped my knuckles on the desk. "I want to report a missing person."

The officer narrowed her eyes and turned her back to say something to her telephone buddy. She hung up the phone and grabbed a clipboard. "Ma'am, how did you say I could help you?"

I read her name on the badge. *Arnetha Pearson*. Didn't I just tell this woman, I wanted to report a missing person?

Could she not hear the desperation in my voice? I cleared my throat and raised my voice, "I said I want to report my daughter missing? Her name is Leesa Patterson."

"No need to raise your voice, ma'am. Your daughter, has she been missing for over twenty-four hours?" The woman narrowed her eyes, which were already slanted and cat-like.

I felt an urge to slap some sense into this woman, standing before me looking like I inconvenienced her. The attitude I could do without. She was the one wearing a blue uniform with an official badge, but I wasn't too sure about her people skills. "Yes, it has been well-over twenty-four hours."

Sgt. Pearson cleared her throat, and pulled a pen from her slicked back bun. "Is she over eighteen?"

"Yes."

"Her name is Lisa Patterson right?"

"It's L-e-e-s-a."

The officer gave me a look and shook her head. That wasn't unusual.

My mother tried being different with my name. Eugena would've been fine. But something about the Eug-e-e-na gave it a bit of distinction. At least I liked to think so.

There wasn't much originality with Junior's name. Another Ralph. Even when Cedric came along, Ralph insisted on using his deceased brother's name. I'd known my brother-in-law for all of two years before he was killed in Vietnam. Ralph loved his older brother with a fierceness that he only bestowed on a few people. Who was I to deny him of naming his second son after his brother?

Now Leesa. She threw both of us for a loop. Fifteen years with only testosterone in the house, after I got over my shock, I was elated with the female addition and proceeded to take charge in naming her too.

"Ma'am, you do know sometimes adults take off on their own and might not want to be found?"

She had a point there, but I had some babies, currently under Louise's care, who really needed their mother. I'd only planned to take in a pooch, not two grandkids, and even the dog wasn't in the picture until a few days ago. Funny, how only last week I was complaining about being lonely. If this was the Lord's idea of teaching me a lesson, he wouldn't hear anymore grumbling from me. "Look, my daughter came by with her children on Saturday night."

"She has children and it was Saturday." The woman raised her eyebrows. "Sounds like she was in need of some babysitting."

I looked at the officer like she fell off the Stupid Truck. "Aren't you supposed to be writing this down or something?"

"Well, she has to be gone for twenty-four hours before...."

"I just told you she's been gone over twenty-four hours. She arrived at my home Saturday night. She's been gone since Sunday morning." I leaned into the counter and I stared at Sgt. Pearson. "Today is Monday afternoon, which I believe is more than enough time to say a person is missing."

"I'm sorry, but I'm going to ask you to calm down so I can get the information down." The officer appeared ready to put her hand on her gun, so I stepped away from the counter before I messed around and got myself shot. I would get the most incompetent employee in the department to help me. Maybe I should have asked Amos to come in for this one. "Is there someone else who can help me?"

"Ma'am, I'm trying to help you. Now has she done this before?"

Here we go. All I needed was to tell this woman yes, Leesa has run away before and she would really not take me seriously.

"Yes, when she was younger she ran away twice. It was a difficult time. Her best friend died and she got caught up with the wrong crowd."

By this time my body shook. There was no way I would breakdown in front of this woman. But I knew the feeling in the pit of my stomach shouldn't be ignored. "Look, I don't know if you are a mother, but I know something is not right. She's been good for several years. A real good mother too."

Had I ever told Leesa how proud I was of her taking care of Kisha? She'd turned her life around. All this time-wasting, I hoped Leesa wasn't in some serious trouble.

"When did you discover her missing?"

Eugeena took a deep breath. This woman was on the slow side. "I woke up Sunday morning and couldn't find her in the house."

Sgt. Pearson's eyebrow shot up again, but came back down. "You said she'd brought her children to you. Had she indicated a length of stay?"

"She did mention she wanted to stay for awhile, I don't know how long. There were clothes for the children ..." I stopped. *The bag with the money. I can't mention that.*

"Ma'am, are you okay?"

"I'm fine. I ..." *What should I say? Should I say something? Maybe this wasn't a good idea.* "It's just that I hadn't seen her in awhile and I know she wouldn't have reached out to me unless she needed help. I need you to find her. She could be in real trouble."

Sgt Pearson nodded and jotted down more information on her clipboard. This woman probably had a picture of Leesa in her mind. I don't like labels. I always wanted to see the good in people, especially my own children. Leesa needed me. She would never come out and say it, but she brought those children to me because I was the one person she knew would care for them.

But children don't fall too far from the tree. From experience, I knew Leesa had inherited the I-will-take-care-of-it-my-way part of my personality. We'd bumped heads enough.

I straightened my shoulders and leveled my eyes on Sgt. Pearson. "Thank you for taking the report. I know what you are going to say next. She's an adult and she could have left on her free will. She didn't. Wherever she is, she's driving an aqua blue Nissan Altima. Here is the last registration I have in my possession for the car."

"Ma'am, we will check local hospitals, traffic reports and other stuff. We will do our best to find her. But you need to be aware she may have taken advantage of the free babysitting opportunity. Is there anything else I need to know?"

"Could you check here in Columbia and the Charleston area? She dropped her children off at my home in Charleston, but she lives here in the city."

"Did you think she returned home?"

"I've been to her apartment. Here is the address." After I gave Sgt. Pearson the information, I added, "I talked to one of her neighbors, she mentioned that my daughter's boyfriend..." *Baby daddy.* "... might have been by looking for her. I don't know this young man, but he sounded like he may have been difficult."

"You think this is a domestic violence incident?"

"I don't know, but the neighbor who lives below her made it seem like they fought a lot. It could have been physical in some cases. Could you talk to her? Her name is Mrs. Hattie."

For the first time since I showed up at the desk, Sgt. Pearson eyes really connected with mine. Maybe the fear seeping through my body had reached my eyes. This was serious to me. More than I knew until that moment.

"She's my only daughter and she's still a baby. Just turned twenty-one."

"Mrs. Patterson, we will do everything we can to find her."

"Thank you." I gripped my pocketbook as though I needed it to hold me up and walked out into the bright sunshine. The sun's rays didn't warm my chilled body.

15

When we returned, I thanked Amos for his assistance and gathered the children from Louise's home. I would like to say I slept well, but visions of my child on the run from the law haunted my dreams. Tuesday morning, I woke up with a new burden on my heart. It was past time to tell the boys about their sister. Well, at least one of them.

If anyone knew where Leesa might be, it would be her brother, Cedric. I knew how much Leesa looked up to him. Despite having a baby sister at age fifteen, he never let on Leesa cramped his style or showed resentment for losing his place as "the baby." He was not the typical middle child. No one expected Cedric to become the other doctor in the family. Out of all my children, Cedric butted heads with Ralph the most. Although he admired Ralph's accomplishments in the medical community, to this day, he refused to visit his father's grave.

"Where are you headed to this morning, Eugeena?" Louise asked me innocently as I handed over my two sleepy grands. As much as I wanted to share my mission with Louise, I had to be wary. If she knew what all had transpired in my household since Saturday evening, I would never get her to keep quiet.

Thirty-five minutes later, after crawling through morning traffic, circling the hospital parking lot, I found a spot. I cut the engine and stared at the glass and concrete structure. I really didn't want to walk in the place. Too many memories. Ralph was this beautiful caramel man with a bright countenance, well-known for having a warm bedside manner with his patients. He was a distinguished obstetrician at the Charleston General Women Center. He loved delivering babies and teaching his residents. This same deeply admired man was a complete stranger to me at times.

Ralph was a good man, who chose to do the right thing, marry a woman pregnant with his child. That woman being me. There were years I wasn't sure if he ever really loved me. Funny in the back of his Chevy Impala, he didn't mind saying the words I needed to hear before I shared my most treasured gift with him. I knew I was head over heels in love with this beautiful man until I started feeling funny. When I told him I thought I might be pregnant, his response left me a shriveled mess. I grew up with no dad around, but my oldest brother made sure to confront the young Ralph Patterson about what he intended to do. It all happened so fast, me married with a baby. After awhile, I wasn't so sure I really loved him either.

I didn't need to think about the past now. God had a way of turning the situation around even after years of what seemed like unanswered prayers. When the first heart attack hit Ralph, it was probably the first time I'd ever truly seen his vulnerable side. It was so ironic the one who held so many young lives in his hands, laid in a hospital bed facing his own immortality.

The experience humbled both of us. Despite all the pockets of misunderstandings that drove us to be more like enemies than friends for so long, our last years together were more beautiful than I could ever imagine. It really did pay to stick it out in a marriage and trust God. God is the fuel that keeps the relationship in drive.

Okay, I needed to find Cedric. I wouldn't have to do this if my son would respond to his voice mail. I'd only left at least ten messages. I moved my derriere from the car and walked up the path towards the hospital's front doors. I smiled at the receptionist. "How are you, honey? I'm Eugeena Patterson, I'm wondering if you could tell me if Dr. Cedric Patterson is with a patient? His mother is looking for him."

"Sure ma'am, let me see if I can locate him for you."

I smiled at her. Really smiled. As a mother I felt good asking for my son. The doctor. Following his dad's footsteps as an obstetrician. With Junior being a lawyer, my heart swelled with pride over my sons.

Then, there was Leesa. An invisible needle burst my bubble. There was hope for her. She was only twenty-one.

"Ma'am, he appears to have several deliveries on the schedule today. Would you like to leave a message?"

"No, that's okay." I rounded the corner and headed toward the elevators. The gift shop enticed me with its assortment of stuffed animals, some fit with helium balloons. I had thought about volunteering at the hospital after I retired, but now with the neighborhood association on my plate, looks like I will be plenty busy.

Plenty busy trying to catch a killer. With all my energy centered on finding Leesa, I could not forget there was an unknown person floating out there that I needed to find to prove my child's innocence.

The elevator doors opened and several people stepped off. I entered with some trepidation. Sometimes riding in the enclosed moving box made me feel like I'd messed around and let somebody trick me into getting on an amusement park ride. I pressed the third floor button. A good cup of coffee from the hospital cafeteria would give me time to think. I had this gut feeling I should be the one to find Leesa first. So I had to look for her in all her spots.

As soon as the elevator door opened, smells from the cafeteria assaulted my nose, making me realize it was close to the lunch hour. A hint of meatloaf and green beans floated through the open double doors. The hospital had remodeled this end of the building, but the cafeteria still looked the same, just now with a huge salad bar plopped in the middle.

I observed the sea of colorful scrubs to find my son, just in case he might have ventured down for some nutrition in between delivering babies. Instead, my eyes caught sight of someone else sitting alone at a table. *Well, what's she doing here?* I grabbed a cup from the dispenser and poured my coffee, then mixed in some Splenda and creamer. With the white lid in place, I maneuvered my hips around the tables to one in the back.

I approached the woman sitting with her head down. She had some white wires coming out of her head. One of those iPod things, I guess. I sat my coffee on the table. "Carmen?"

The young woman lifted her eyes, and then adjusted her torso in the seat from her previous slumped position. "Mrs. Patterson, hey how are you?"

I pointed to the seat. "Do you mind if I sit with you for awhile?"

"No, please do." She frowned. "Is someone you know staying at the hospital?"

"No, no. What about you?"

"Just off my shift. Second-year resident."

"Well, I'll be, I did not know. I was just talking to Mr. Amos about how much I didn't know about some of our neighbors. Can't be too careful, you know?"

She raised her eyebrows at me.

Maybe that came out wrong.

Carmen sat back in the seat and crossed her arms. "Well, I don't have anything to hide. Just trying to get through this residency."

"Oh I was just running my mouth. Don't mind me."

She continued to stare like she wasn't too sure about me. "People do like their privacy."

"That's true, but with all that's happened, it might be a good idea for the neighbors to reach out to each other. You were at the last neighborhood association, right? I'm sure you remember us talking about this."

Carmen uncrossed her arms. "Yeah, you're right. I guess we probably should try to know each other better especially with what happened to Mrs. Fleming. Have you heard anymore about the investigation?"

"No, I haven't. I guess it's all down to the evidence stuff. You know like on *CSI*."

"Yeah. The forensics. Fingerprints and fiber. All that stuff does take awhile."

I nodded as silence settled between us despite the conversations going on around us. I still wasn't quite sure what to think of Carmen. She was on my list of mystery folks. Her defensiveness a minute ago piqued my curiosity. I sipped some of my coffee. *Smooth and strong.* "This is good." I lifted my cup. "I have no business drinking it."

"Why, what's happened?"

"Chile, diabetes happened."

"Is that why you started walking? Exercise and diet can really help maintain your glucose levels."

Okay, sistah girl kept up with me walking, but a minute ago she seemed resistant to the whole getting to know *you* bit. I pointed my index finger in her direction. "You sound like a doctor already young lady."

The hardness of Carmen's jaw softened as a slight smile appeared. "Thanks. I have a long way to go. I want to be an obstetrician."

"You do? I'm sure my son can help you out."

Carmen blinked, the smile disappeared. "Your son works here?"

"You can't miss him, chile. That boy is not one to be ignored. Believe me, I'm his mama. Dr. Patterson. Cedric

Patterson." I observed Carmen's face. A range of emotions etched across her pretty face. "Carmen, are you okay?"

"I'm fine. I guess I never made the connection. You know that you were Cedric's mother."

First name basis? Since when was a resident that cozy with the attending physician? "So, you do know each other?"

"Yes. I report to him."

I wanted to poke my nose further into this revelation, but Carmen jumped up from the table. Her headphones went flying around her neck. "You know what? I need to get going."

My goodness, she had to be close to six feet if not over. She probably could look Cedric right in the eyes. I strained my neck looking up at her from the table. "Didn't you just get off your shift?"

"I did, but I have a lot to do today. Nice talking with you."

"Okay." I doubt Carmen heard me as she whizzed out of the cafeteria like her scrubs were on fire. I could only deal with one child's mess at a time. When the time was right, Cedric would have to explain what he did to my neighbor. Most importantly I wanted to know more about this young woman and what she knew about the Patterson family.

16

I knew as soon as she opened the door, Louise wasn't about to let me off the hook. As I entered her home, it always struck me as odd how similar our houses were constructed on the inside. Now the decor was another matter. Being a social studies teacher, I loved history and especially loved exploring my family tree. Photos of family members as far back to 1890 graced my hallway along with school photos of my children.

Now Louise was the cat lady of Sugar Creek. I remember her having as many as a half dozen cats at one time. In the house. Now only two remained. There were no signs of the sleek grey cat, Sylvester but the old tabby, Chester, sat perched on a chair, keeping an eye on me. There were more than just the live cats. There was the cat wallpaper. The cat figurines. The cat wall hangings. The cat rug. And yes, Louise was sporting one of her probably hundred shirts with a feline imprinted on the front.

Louise shuffled into the living room. "We had a good time. Miss Kisha is so sweet."

Kisha sat on the couch, her eyes glued to the television. When she saw me, she ran over. "Grandma. Did your bring Mama?"

Oh Lord, here we go.

Louise picked up Tyric from the carrier. "Yeah, Eugeena. Where is Leesa?"

This must be how a cornered cat felt except there was no way I could scratch my way out of this one. But I had no answers for either one of them. I still tried to get my head wrapped around the fact that my child dropped her kids off Saturday night and hasn't been seen since. And the new grandbaby, well I just laid that burden down at Jesus' feet. The child was here now and that story would have to come later.

"Let me get Tyric." He really was a good baby. Leesa hadn't given me much trouble during her baby years either. "With two little ones Leesa needed a bit of a break. I remember when Junior and Cedric were about their ages; I thought I would pull my hair out." At least I prayed that's what this situation was all about. She would show up rested and with a full explanation for her disappearance. Then, all would be back to normal.

Maybe not. There still was the problem of a dead neighbor whose funeral was only two days away.

"Louise, I did need to ask you something that's been worrying me."

"Sure, is it about Mary? I'm telling you I'm getting most of my sleep during the daytime. Can't bear to close my eyes when the sun goes down."

I didn't think Louise liked to keep her eyes off much of anything at anytime of the day. "We need to discuss some strategies on how to get to know our neighbors."

"You're right about that. Most of the folks around here are young. I sure hated to see Clarissa passing a year ago and Johnny's daughter moved him up to North Carolina with her. I heard she put him in a nursing home anyway."

I shook my head. I still had years on me to enjoy my home, but I knew a day would come when I might be shipped off to a nursing home or to live with one of my kids. As much as I whined about loneliness, I wanted to keep my independence more. Staying healthy would be even more important. I looked down to find Tyric studying my face, while holding his finger in his mouth. I also needed to keep my energy level up so I could enjoy my grandkids.

"Louise, do you know anything about Carmen? Seeing she lives on the other side of you."

She clasped her hands together. "Pretty girl, but certainly a strange one."

"How so?"

"She was one of the first to get robbed you know?"

"What? Carmen never said anything about her house being robbed?"

"She didn't report it the police."

"You are kidding, right? Please tell me how you know?"

"I went by her house one morning after I heard all this racket the night before. I wanted to check on her. Neighborly thing to do, right? Anyhow, she opened the door, but she didn't invite me in. But from where I stood I could tell the place had been ransacked or either honey doesn't clean her house very well. Plus she seemed really upset about her laptop being missing."

"She told you someone stole it?"

"Well, no. She just said they took the laptop, but she was kind of talking to herself. She really was kind of out of it. Like she was in shock."

Not really sure whether to believe Louise's tale or not, "I just saw her at the hospital. Did you know she was a resident over there?"

"I figured she must have worked at the hospital. She comes in and out of her home all times of night and she wears scrubs."

"How long has she been next door anyway?"

"She moved in a few months after Johnny's folks moved him out. If I'm not mistaken I think she knew the family or they were familiar with her."

"So, she's from North Carolina. A relative?"

By this time Kisha was pulling on my skirt. "Grandma, I'm hungry."

"Hold just a minute, honey. We will be home soon." I hoped to hear back from Cedric soon. Seeing Carmen's reaction about him earlier, I might can get some more out of him. "Have you noticed if anyone has been in and out of her house?"

"You sure have a lot of questions about this woman all of a sudden."

"Well, we did just have a murder here at Sugar Creek. We need to find out more about the people around us. Don't you think?"

Louise rubbed her hands through her thinning silver hair. "That's the truth. You know that I hate to stick my nose where he doesn't belong, but she does get male company at night."

Oh oh. I steeled myself by bowing my head down. Cedric was quite the ladies man, but surely he wouldn't be down the street with a young neighbor so close to his own mama's house.

"Wayne. He's been over there quite a bit."

I whipped my head back up, almost putting a cramp in my neck. "Wayne Goodman from across the street? Carmen and Wayne?"

"Yep. I seen him show up at her house late in the evening. A few times."

"They're seeing each other? I would think they weren't each other's type." I thought back to the neighborhood meeting a few weeks back. When they were at my house I remember they sat on opposite sides of the living room. Seemed pretty indifferent to me. Almost like they couldn't care less to be in the same room with each other. Was that a ploy to hide something? "What's the story on Wayne anyway?"

"He served time, but for what I don't know. You remember Clarissa was really hush-hush about the whole situation. Her broken heart probably took her to an early grave."

"I can maybe ask Amos to check it out. He mentioned we need to be aware of folks around here with police records."

"That sounds like a plan. Eugeena, you know you sounding like a detective over there. If I didn't know any better, I would think you are trying to figure this out yourself? And what's going on with you and Amos?"

"Nothing."

Louise smiled. "I think you two make a great couple."

"What? Please woman," I stuttered. The last thing I needed was Louise trying to play matchmaker. There were more things on my plate to worry about than my love life.

I gathered the children and headed towards the door. Another question struck me. "Have you heard anyone saying they saw somebody around Mary's house on Friday night?"

"No, but I imagine they are not going to get anywhere without a witness."

I needed to find this witness. Hopefully, Amos would have some luck picking Detective Wilkes for information. "Kisha, give Ms. Louise a hug. Thanks for watching them, Louise." Kisha skipped down the sidewalk. "Grandma, can I play with Porky?"

"Who? Oh you mean Porgy. Of course, sugar. I'm sure after being lonesome, he will love to play."

"Can we play in the yard?"

"It's too hot right now. Hurry up so we can get inside."

What in the world? Did I hear my name?

I turned around. Tamara waved from across the street. I waved back.

Is she coming over? Oh, yes she is.

"Hi, Miss Eugeena. You out walking with the grandkids today?"

"Actually, we're trying to get out of this hot sun." I peered into Tamara's face. Her eyes were red. "Are you okay, honey?"

"I'm fine. Just missing Melvin. I tried to call him and I guess he's still in a meeting."

Against my better judgment, I felt sorry for the woman. I knew too well about a man being too busy with his work to come home or remember his family. Really, if that man planned to stay married, he needed to pay more attention to his wife. "Why don't you join us? I'm going to get dinner started."

"I can barely cook rice. Maybe I can learn some tips from you." Tamara grinned big and wide. She had straight white teeth.

"Sure, come on inside. Now a Paula Deen I am not, but I can show you some basics." Back before the doctor made me change my cooking habits, I might have given ole Paula from the Food Network Channel some competition with my fried chicken.

"May I hold your grandson?" The girl held out her arms, looking woefully at Tyric. "I can't wait to have a baby one day."

Lord, if you expected me to mentor this young wife and I can't keep up with my own daughter, certainly I wasn't the one with godly advice to give. One thing I knew for sure, children added a whole other level to a relationship. "Girl, don't rush yourself. Let God time the entrance of children into your life. Now let's go inside. This child needs to be changed."

Porgy barked and yipped so when I came through the door with the children, I thought he would have a stroke. I put him upstairs with the children. Tamara didn't know she was going to be put to work when I came back into the kitchen. I pulled out pots and would have made Rachel Ray proud with the way I chopped and stirred all the while grilling my kitchen guest.

"Tell me how long have you been married, Tamara?"

"One year yesterday."

"Really? Well, what did you do to celebrate?"

Tamara wouldn't look at me. I had her chopping onions, but I wasn't so sure if the tear that rolled down her face was from the onions or something else. She finally answered, "Melvin had to be out of town so we will celebrate this weekend."

Well, that explained the source of Tamara's tears earlier. This was not the way to start off a marriage. "I'm sure Melvin will have something extra special planned."

"I don't know. We've been fighting so much lately. He's pretty upset with me."

"It will blow over. Just give him time. Sometime a man's pride stops him from seeing straight."

Tamara walked over to the stove and raked the onions into the skillet. When she turned around, her face was so distraught. I would have hugged her but my hands were covered with flour. "Chile, sit down and rest yourself. Being married is hard work, but don't give up. With thirty-five years of marriage under my belt, I can tell you I had to learn to pray and trust God."

"I'm not really on good terms with God, Miss Eugeena. Probably now more than ever. I went to your church Sunday because ... things just keep going from bad to worse. I don't know what to do."

"Well, attending church is a start. As long as you are seeking God that's what matters. You don't ever want to just go through life not trying to connect to the Lord at all. He's always trying to reach us. The communication usually stops because we don't respond."

"So, you believe God really does forgive you for anything?"

"It says it in his Word. I'm no bible expert, but I believe what the Scriptures say." I knew this was one of those moments that came along where you're supposed to witness. I went over to the sink to rinse my hands. I grabbed the kitchen towel and walked up beside Tamara, "Would you like a relationship with God?"

"I ... I have some things that need to be fixed."

"Oh no, chile. You come to Jesus just as you are. Let him fix it."

"Thank you, Miss Eugeena. I will think about it some more."

"Eugeena. You can call me Eugeena." I patted her on the arm. "I will be here if you need to talk some more. Why don't you grab the lettuce out the fridge over there? You can chop some up in that big bowl."

I wasn't sure if my talk helped any. You can't make anyone accept Jesus. My youngest son and daughter, despite all the Sunday school, were still on the fence. I planted the seed and that's all that God required. It still hurt my heart to know people, especially loved ones, didn't truly know the Lord.

Lord, where was Leesa's heart with you? My child, my child.

17

Tamara's presence in the kitchen made me miss Leesa all the more. My daughter never did like sitting around in the kitchen. Explains why she never learned how to do anything but boil eggs.

"Mmm, Miss Eugeena this pork chop is so good." Tamara licked her fingers.

"Glad you like it. I sure get tired of chicken breasts." I looked at the clock on the microwave wondering if I should call Cedric again. He should have gotten one of my messages by now. That boy could be just a bad as his father with being in his own world. I know he was all about delivering babies, but right now I needed him to possibly help save his sister's life.

"Is something bothering you?"

I smiled at Tamara, who peered into my face with concern. "I'm fine. Just a little frustrated by everything that's happened."

She put her fork down. "You mean about Mrs. Fleming."

"Yes. Sugar Creek is an old neighborhood. We've had our ups and downs, but in the thirty years I've been here, never a murder."

"It is truly horrible. I guess most folks are afraid now."

"Well, this has shaken up quite a few of us. But don't you worry. Enjoy your meal. Anytime you need me, I'm here. We will all look out for each other."

I looked over at Kisha's dinner plate. Just like her mama. A plate full of green beans. "Honey, eat some of your vegetables." Kisha scrunched her little nose up and looked down at her plate.

I stopped chewing my pork chop and cocked my ear toward the kitchen doorway. My front door lock just clicked. I rose from the table. By the time I made my way through the living room, the front door flew open.

"Ma, what smells so good in here?" The tall, caramel man standing in front of me, birthed from my womb thirty-five years before was the spitting image of his deceased father. I walked over to Cedric and hugged him fiercely. "It's about time."

"Whoa, Ma you're going to break a rib with that hug." He pulled back and smiled a perfect set of white teeth thanks to two years of braces. Probably out of all the kids, Cedric had the most awkward stages. Gawky and geeky looking all at the same time. Somewhere around sixteen, he caught up to his older brother and filled out, inheriting his dad's relaxed curls.

"Why is it when I need your help, you can never be found?"

"Hey, I'm here now. Let's see what you got going on in the kitchen." Cedric walked ahead of me, turning up his sleeves. "Is that little Kisha? Come here, how's my favorite girl?" He scooped his niece up in his arms.

Through giggles, Kisha shouted, "Uncle Ceddy."

My heart dipped at the sight. I so wanted Cedric to settle down and find a good woman. He would make a great dad. A definite natural with kids. "Cedric, let me fix you a plate."

"Sure. And who might this lovely lady be? You didn't tell me you had company." Cedric put his niece down and held his hand out towards Tamara.

A glow had crept around the girl's beautiful dark brown cheeks. "Uh excuse me." I stepped in front of Cedric, to protect poor Tamara. "This is a neighbor. A married one."

He looked back at Tamara and flashed her one of his megawatt smiles with absolutely no shame. "Sometimes Mama likes to play matchmaker. I can never be too sure."

Of course he was right. I had tried to help him settled down on a number occasions with some good Christian woman.

Tamara laughed. "You have a great mother." She placed her napkin on the table and stood. "Miss Eugeena, thanks for the meal."

"Anytime, let me walk you out." On the way out the kitchen, I could hear Cedric sending Kisha into a fit of giggles again.

"Remember, you call me anytime you want to talk, you hear?"

Tamara teared up a little. "Thank you. I appreciate you being so nice to me."

I watched her until she had arrived safely across the street. There really were a lot of women in this neighborhood who lived or spent a lot of time alone. This would be a topic to address at the neighborhood meeting coming up soon. We might be able to get a self-defense class started. Now that would be something else.

Me and my stubby legs trying to kickbox.

I put Kisha in the room with Porgy so I could talk to her uncle alone.

Cedric looked up from the table when I entered the kitchen. "Where's that barking coming from? You have a dog in the house?"

"You don't know do you? Mary died three days ago."

Unlike his older brother and his mama, Cedric had the kind of skin that would turn red in a hot minute. "What? How? When?"

"I was walking Saturday and something told me to check on her. She was…on her kitchen floor. Gone."

"You found her ... like that?"

"Yes, which is why I need your help? I need to find your sister."

Cedric frowned. "Why?"

"Leesa came the Saturday night with the kids. It sounded like she was in trouble, but we never had a chance to talk. I woke up Sunday morning, she was gone."

"No, she didn't?" Cedric let out a long sigh. "Mama, you don't need to be taking care of Kisha."

"Kisha and Tyric are fine with me."

"Tyric? She had the baby already."

Something slipped out of Cedric's mouth that caused my ears to burn. I smacked him on the arm. "There is no need for *that* language. You already knew about the baby?"

"I'm sorry Ma. I told her to tell you. She just showed up with him out of the blue?"

"I don't want to go into that now. Something is wrong. Don't make that face at me. I am a mother and you are not."

Cedric placed his arm around my shoulders. "Mama, don't do this. She's probably fine."

I swallowed. "I need you to look out for your sister. Check the hospitals. I already filed a missing persons report."

"You really think something happened?"

"This is more than a mother's instinct. This detective on Mary's case says she has some kind of witness that saw Leesa at Mary's house the night she died."

Cedric sucked in his breath. "You have got to be kidding me? What in the world did that girl do now?"

"We don't know if she did anything." I decided that it would not be a good time to tell Cedric about the money in the closet.

"Cedric, since you knew about the baby, then you must know who she was seeing. Who's the father?"

"I don't know. I saw her with some guy a few months ago at Club Magic. Ma, you don't have to scrunch up your face like that? You know neither Leesa nor I are sanctified like you and Junior."

That's alright; I kept both of them prayed up. "Did you catch the man's name?"

"It was Chris something. I didn't really talk to him other than to say hello. I had other things on my mind than keeping an eye on my little sister."

"Oh really. Like what?"

"Ma, you don't want to know. Look I will be on the lookout for her. Did you try her on her cell phone, by the way?"

"I tried the number I had, but it said it was out of service."

"I think she has a new number, hold on."

Cedric whipped out his fancy, smancy phone. One of those iPhones. The gadget reminded me of the one I saw Carmen with at the hospital earlier. Looked like they had a few things in common. I watched him glide his fingertips across the smooth surface and scrolled through what looked like a lot of numbers. This must be the new black book.

"Here we go. This is the last number I have for her. Let me try it. I got plenty to say to her."

"Just tell her to get back here." I crossed my arms and watched his face. When he grunted, I assumed he didn't get her.

"Leesa, girl where are you? You got Mama all worried. Get back here and get your kids."

I shook my head. Despite Ralph being gone, with two brothers, Leesa had two other "fathers" on her case.

"Mama, she'll probably be back soon." Cedric helped himself to another helping of food. After he sat back down, I decided to hit him with another question just as he wrapped his mouth around the pork chop.

"Is Carmen Alpine one of your residents?"

Cedric dropped the bone and blinked his eyes as though he was thinking hard. Really hard. "Carmen? How do you know her?"

"She's a neighbor, been living on the other side of Louise in Johnny Calvin's house."

Cedric blew out a breath. "I didn't know that."

"Didn't know she lived down the street from me? What did you do to her anyway?"

He held his hands up in the air. "What are you accusing me of doing?"

"Carmen had a rather negative reaction when I mentioned your name. Any reasons why? She's a tad bit too young for you."

"Whoa, whoa. I know you like to think I'm the biggest flirt on the planet, but I have not bothered Carmen. If anything she's probably a little disappointed I haven't taken her offers. I'm pretty strict about not messing with residents. Strictly professional."

So, Carmen was sweet on my son? No wonder it didn't help to find out his mother lived down the street. "Well, what do you know about her?"

"Carmen?"

"No Charmin. Boy, tell me about the woman. She's been my neighbor for a few months now and I don't know anything about her."

"What's wrong with that? I don't know most of my neighbors either?"

"Cedric?"

"I don't know much about Carmen. She's from North Carolina. I believe she mentioned being an Army brat. Her parents settled down in Columbia on their last assignment at Fort Jackson. She graduated from Clemson and then attended the Medical University of Carolina. That's all I know."

Cedric picked his plate up off the table, scraped the remains and brought it over to the sink. I had to grin as I watched him stick his hands into my soapy dish water. I trained my boys well. There was no such thing as boys not washing dishes in my house.

I picked up the other dishes off the table and carried them over to the sink. "Army brat. That explains some things. Didn't Wayne go into the army after graduation?"

Cedric leaned against the fridge and crossed his arms. "Yeah, he served in Desert Storm. He was discharged after that. I haven't really kept up with him in years. Why are you asking?"

I rinsed the dishes and said over my shoulder, "According to Louise, Wayne and Carmen are good friends."

Cedric laughed, "Well you can't listen to everything Louise says. I mean Carmen wouldn't have anything in common with Wayne. I mean Wayne. Please."

"Are you trying to convince me or you?" I turned around to catch Cedric staring off into space. "Are you okay?"

He waved his arm like he was swatting a fly. "Yeah. I'm fine. Look I need to go."

I followed him to the front door. "Cedric, do you know if Leesa had any reason to talk to Mary in the past few weeks?"

"Now that you mentioned it Leesa did call me a week ago. I think Mary sent her a package. Something that belonged to Jenny."

Jenny, Mary's daughter, had died during Leesa's junior year. "Why would she give Leesa something belonging to Jenny, especially five years after her death?"

"Leesa mentioned something about Mary was going to give whatever it was to Jenny on her twenty-first birthday. I guess she wanted Leesa to have it since she just turned twenty-one."

That was sweet and so like the Mary I used to know. It also shot another dagger in my heart, because that presented the possibility that Leesa had been near or even inside Mary's house the night she was killed.

18

Little creatures had taken over my home. Not long after Cedric left, Kisha and Tyric reminded me why I never liked the idea of grand young'uns staying over past three day. Never again would I whine to the Lord about loneliness. Me, God, Jesus and the Holy Spirit would be just fine. Now Mr. Porgy could become a permanent resident as soon as we got this sleeping thing down. I had to keep the bedroom doors closed because as soon as I turned my back, the little four-legged wonder would find him a bed to lay his shaggy self. How he managed to climb with his little legs was a mystery.

"Grandma, can Porgy stay in the bed with me?"

"No honey. You and Tyric don't need the dog in here while you sleep. Everyone has their own bed."

"But Porgy looks so sad."

"Well, he lost somebody special to him, but I know he appreciates you playing with him."

"I wish Mama would let us have a dog. She said Mrs. Hattie don't like animals."

My ears perked up. "You like Mrs. Hattie?"

"Yes, she watches me when Mama goes to work. Sometimes her and mama yell at each other."

"Is that so?" That reminded me of the man Chris. "Kisha, what about Chris? Does your mama talk loud with him to?"

Kisha's eyes grew wide.

"Kisha."

"He hit me. Mama yelled at him."

I shrunk back. "He hit you?"

She nodded and held up her arm. "Right here." Kisha pointed to her forearm.

I examined her tiny arm. There didn't appear to be any recent marks, but the fact that this unknown man laid his hands on my grandchild spiked my blood pressure. "Come here, baby." I wrapped my arms around her and then tucked the covers around her body real tight. I wondered if Leesa ran off to get away from this Chris fellow. My daughter being missing may not have anything to do with Mary's death.

I peeked at Tyric in the playpen. The temporary bedding would have to do until I could figure out a better place to put him. Thank goodness I had the playpen stored away in the closet from when Junior's twins visited when they were younger.

I left the nightstand lamp burning and shuffled down the hallway. Just as I reached my bedroom door, the phone rang. I grabbed the cordless phone from the nightstand. "Hello."

"Eugeena, you doing alright over there?"

"Hey Cora. I'm so glad to hear your voice. I just put the children to bed."

"Oh good! I was calling to find out when Mary's funeral will be? I would like to drive up to give you some support."

Mary's funeral.

"Cora, I've been caught up trying to track Leesa down. I believe the pastor said her family arranged the funeral services for Thursday. Speaking of the funeral, Pastor Jones had asked me to speak on behalf of the church. Cora, what can I say?"

"Plenty. Look, I know you were a bit pig-headed about the incident a few years back, but you have to put that behind you. You more than anyone knew Mary best."

I knew Cora was right. Didn't stop me from feeling like a hypocrite though. "Thanks, Cora. I appreciate you."

"I will drive down Thursday morning and meet you at the church. Don't worry about Leesa. That child has always been resourceful and you know God has had his hands on her since birth."

We both said goodbye and I hung up the phone. I kept feeling like I was missing something.

I headed towards the closet and opened the door. Did I pull everything out of the diaper bag? I emptied the contents of the bag on my bed. The diapers had long been removed. I unfolded two rolls of money. One appeared to be almost five hundred dollars while the other one was near a thousand. *Where did you get this money, Leesa?* I rummaged through the other items. Baby lotion and baby wipes. I sniffed cherry flavored lip gloss mixed in. Even with young children, my daughter still kept her appearance up. I unzipped the side part of the bag.

Well, I'll be.

I pulled out the bible, a gift from me to Leesa, when she turned thirteen years old. I had her name engraved in gold on the front cover. It really pleased me that Leesa had it in her possession. I rubbed the white leather, and turned the bible over in my hand. An envelope stuck out the back.

I removed the envelope and flipped it over. It had been a long time, but I recognized the loopy "L." The envelope was postdated May 12th. That was the day after Mother's Day.

Mary had mailed this envelope to Leesa about three weeks ago.

I pulled out the stationary recognizing another familiarity. Mary loved her lavender scent. My hands shook as I unfolded the letter. This could have been the last piece of correspondence my old friend had sent. I wasn't sure what it all meant.

My eyes took in the Dearest Leesa part and jumped down into the letter.

You are probably wondering why I'm writing you this letter. It's been a long time and past due. You know every time I see your mother, and I see her often now walking in the morning, I think about how things used to be. How you used to come and spend the night with Jennifer and you two would giggle into the morning hours. I hate how things fell apart years ago and even more so not having Jennifer here. You know she would be 21 now. I know you are all grown up and I often imagine if things had worked out differently, you two would be talking about your careers, marriages and children.

Anyway to get to the point of this letter. I'm sorry about the grief brought to you years ago. I probably should have told you, but I found that ring. The one that was so precious and I went berserk because it went missing. To this day, I don't know Jennifer's reasoning. She and I didn't get along so often. Out in public we smiled, but we barely spoke to each other. I wondered if she did it to spite me although I don't know why she included you in her scheme.

That ring was in her jewelry box, well hidden. I found it as I cleaned her things out. It so broke me down because I had planned to give her that ring on her 21st birthday. But she's not here.

I don't know if God is speaking to me, but I felt like you should have the ring. You can do whatever you want with it, but I wanted you to have it. I know it won't change the past, but I hope it may allow an opportunity for me to see you again. I also hope one day your mother would forgive me for fighting her so hard when she stood by your innocence.

Sincerely yours always,

Mary

A lump took over my airways. I knew it. I knew it. My daughter was innocent. All this time. *Mary, why didn't you come forward and tell the truth?*

I knew God aimed to make things right between Mary and me. Those times I walked by her house. That burning desire to do more than wave hello. The Holy Spirit urged me to do more, to take the first step towards reconciliation.

Neither one of us had obeyed.

I wept.

19

It was Wednesday. The day before Mary was to be buried. Over three days and no sign of Leesa, I prayed with all my might that Detective Wilkes had found some other leads in the case. I envisioned her wanting to show up at the house with a search warrant. How would I explain the money? Not including the letter from Mary? Circumstantial evidence, right?

It did occur to me that Leesa could have retrieved the ring from Mary and pawned it. That would explain the money. Would my daughter strike out at Mary in anger after learning the truth of the ring? I was a bit peeved myself that Mary kept that secret so long.

The past was what it was. I had the present to contend with.

Early in the morning, I had heard Amos outside making a racket with some obnoxious tool, possibly a saw. I meant to ask him the other day what he was doing with all that lumber in the backyard. For the past few weeks, it appeared he was putting together a shed. I decided to walk over and see if he had a chance to get any information from Wilkes. If Amos had offered to hold my hand, I would have let him. Lord, it's been that kind of a week. For some reason the man brought a deep comfort to me.

Before I could get two feet up the walkway to Amos' front porch, I looked up to see someone walking towards me. "Wayne?"

The young man stopped mid-stride. "Uh, hey, Miss Eugeena. How you doing this morning?"

I wanted to ask him the same. More so I wanted to know what happened to him. The scruffy braids were replaced with a low haircut to the scalp. Wayne even shaved off the beard he'd been sporting. "Well, you look awfully handsome this morning. You got you a girl or something?"

Wayne laughed. "Wow, Miss Eugeena, you don't change. Always say what's on your mind. Let's just say I've had a new outlook on life."

I cocked my eyebrow, remembering Louise's reports of seeing Wayne with Carmen. As Wayne walked away, I called out to his back. "Your mama would be proud."

He stopped for a minute, but didn't turn around. I watched him cross the street, feeling a bit bad about my suspicions. Or should I? Just because a person suddenly cleaned up didn't let them off the hook.

Amos definitely had a saw churning again. I waited until he stopped and then called to him, "Amos, when you ready to take a break, come over for some lunch."

He broke out into a grin. "I'll be there."

About an hour later, I walked out to the front porch with a tray of turkey sandwiches and ice tea. Kisha and Porgy tore around the front yard like two loose cannons. Tyric enjoyed yet another good nap in his carrier. His mouth was turned up into a smile, his little chubby cheeks appeared healthy and glowing. What I wouldn't do to trade places with him. Before I could join Amos for lunch, the phone rang.

I barely greeted the caller before they spurted out, "Is that girl back yet?"

Lawd, Jesus! I rolled my eyes up to the heavens. "Hello to you too, Junior." I must have skipped the lesson on phone etiquette with my oldest child. Come to think of it, I skipped around on a lot of lessons among the three of these young'uns.

"Mama, I'm so sorry that girl is putting you through these changes again."

Junior didn't have any concept of keeping his cool. "Sounds like you talked to Cedric."

"You don't have to worry about a thing, Mama. We'll be up there this weekend."

"What?" What does this boy mean by "we"?

"Ralph, Jr. I don't really need a house full of people right now. Since you talked to your brother, then you know about Mary's passing."

"Yeah, that's another reason why we're coming. Mama, you can't stay in that house by yourself anymore."

"Excuse me." I just about had enough of this. *Lord, I won't complain no more.* "I am not leaving my home. I have lived here for over thirty years ..."

"Hey, did she run off with that dude?"

Dude? Junior's mixture of Anglo-Saxon, surfer boy talk stumped me. This time it flat out caused me to pause. "What *dude?*"

"I remember seeing her a few months ago with some guy."

"You did?" *How did these boys know more about Leesa's social life than me?* "Well, what did he look like?"

"I know he was looking all crazy because I walked up on them. I told him I was her brother and he better be treating her right."

I had to carefully ask my next question. "How did Leesa seem around him?"

"I don't think she wanted us to really talk. Why? Mama, what's going on?"

"Would you by any chance remember his name?"

"Are you sure you don't need..."

"His name, Junior. Think." I needed to find out who this man was and if he had anything to do with my daughter's disappearing act.

"Chris. Chris Goodman. Chris Golden. I don't know. I just know it was Chris. Oh hold on a minute, Mother."

Mother. It sounded like he was talking to someone else in the background. "Junior. Junior?"

"I've got to go. I have a client waiting for me."

I stared at the phone, the dial tone blared at me. I can't believe that boy.

I joined Amos on the porch. He'd tilted Tyric's carrier a little closer to our chairs to keep the sunlight from touching his sleeping body. His turkey sandwich had been demolished, not a crumb left. "Do you want any more ice tea?"

"No, I'm good. You sit and rest a bit. I know you have to be stressed."

He was right about that, but stressed wasn't the word. I have never had a panic attack, but the queasiness crawling in my stomach couldn't be good. I tapped my foot and let the rocking chair sooth me.

"I tell you that little girl and dog is having themselves a good time out there. Kind of reminds me of my childhood playing outside this time of day."

I peered at him. "Where did you grow up, Amos?"

"Right here in South Carolina. Up the coast, a little further north, in Marion County."

"Oh, I know those little towns in there."

"Where did you grow up?"

"Me? Right here in Charleston. Born and raised. Ralph and I moved to North Charleston while the boys were in elementary school. Been here in Sugar Creek ever since."

"That is a long time."

"Oh yeah. It's funny now, but I remember the day Louise came over while I was cleaning the house. She wanted to know if I worked as I maid. I looked at her and told her I was looking for one myself."

Amos threw his head back and laughed. "Well, you two seem like good buddies now."

"Once you get to know people, you find people are just that…people."

"Sounds like you got quite a bit of history here."

I smiled. History. Some good and some not-too-good. "It's been a blessing to live in Sugar Creek. A lot of folks left over the years, but this has been a place for middle class families to grow and get to know each other. Things changed after the eighties as they built up more around this area."

Kisha and Porgy climbed up on the porch, both out of breath and a bit dusty. I looked over at Amos and saw him peering down at Tyric. "Would be nice to feel that type of peace all the time, huh?"

"You right about that. Little fellow has it made in the shade so to speak." Amos nodded in Kisha's direction who somehow had managed to put Amos' hat on her head. She looked up at us both and gave us a toothy, sweet grin. Would've made a pretty photo if I had one of those digital cameras.

"Kisha, give Mr. Amos his hat back."

"Ah, she ain't hurting it." He turned back to me. His eyes seemed bright and young despite the deep caramel wrinkles in his face. "What can I do to help?"

Earlier I had expressed my fears about this unknown man in Leesa's life to Amos. I shook my head, "Maybe I'm over-reacting. If she would just show up. I've been just about to tear my hair out." I didn't need to be ripping out no hair follicles. I wasn't trying to sport the bald look like Amos.

"Well, I'm sure she has her reasons. It does sound suspicious about this boyfriend though. Maybe she needs to lay low from him for a while."

"I can tell he's not a nice man." Kisha's confession of being struck on the arm by this Chris person didn't sit too well with me.

I still hadn't told Amos about the money in the diaper bag, the letter and the ring. It started to sink in that maybe Leesa was trying to escape or run away from someone. Pondering a million scenarios, none of them good, was making it difficult to keep my composure. Water filled my eyes. I brushed my sleeve across my face as though I was wiping sweat from my brow.

I don't know if Amos noticed my teary eyes. If he did, he was a gentleman about it, by changing the subject. "By the way, I had a talk with Wayne this morning."

I narrowed my eyes. "Yeah, I saw him. He was all cleaned up."

"He actually told me he's been asking other folks about what they'd seen. Apparently, he's concerned about the recent robberies too."

"I bet. Did you find out about anymore about his police record?"

"Just an assault and battery a few years ago. Sounds like in a drunken stupor he got into a fight at some pool place. He was lucky. Most folks are packin' these days."

"Packing?"

"You know, carrying a gun on them."

"Oh." It certainly was a different world.

"Anyhow, Wayne seems to be pretty clean now, but it's still hard for him working in construction especially now the way the market is doing. You know this housing boom and all the foreclosures gave everyone a beating finance-wise."

"I know, it's a shame." I'd been suspicious of Wayne, but the fact is the witness still pointed out seeing a woman at Mary's house. "Amos, what about the witness? Any ideas?"

He shook his head. "Detective Wilkes has been pretty closed mouth. She especially wasn't too keen to share anything. She's the only female detective and certainly didn't want to hear from an old pro like me."

A car caught my attention as it pulled into the driveway across the street. I recognized Tamara's husband BMW. "I hope mister over there came home to make up for missing the anniversary. That's not the way to keep a woman happy."

"I guess my wife would've said the same thing if she was here." Amos rubbed his chin, his eyes focused on nothing in particular, except whatever memory that flowed through his mind. "It wasn't until I got shot, lying in a hospital bed, I looked up to see her standing over me, I realized how much of my life I missed. Children all grown and my beautiful bride had become almost a stranger."

I whipped my head around at the mention of Amos, using the word stranger. What really struck me was Ralph and I had a similar situation, with Ralph suffering a heart attack. Did folks really need God to get their attention quite so dramatically? I commented, "You were so devoted to her during her cancer treatments."

"I owed her. When that cancer tore through her body, I would have done anything to trade places with her."

My eyes filled with tears again. It's something special to see how God matures a person to really see what life is all about.

Amos stood suddenly, sending the rocking chair into a frenzy of motion. "Eugeena, I think you should plan to call an emergency neighborhood association meeting. Can you round up folks by Friday evening?"

"That's pretty short notice."

"You want to find that witness? You might even have some suspects show up."

I shot an uneasy look at Amos. "Are you saying I could be inviting a murderer to my house?"

"From my experience, whoever did it, if they are from around here, they will show up to see what others are saying, you know make sure they are in the clear. Another place to keep an eye out for anything suspicious will be the funeral tomorrow."

"That's kind of bold to show up to the person's funeral?"

"It is, but people do some crazy stuff in the heat of the moment. I mean think about Cain and Abel. When God came looking, Cain was all nonchalant, like it was no big deal that he took his brother's life."

There was a lot about Amos I didn't know. Him getting all biblical on me was a bit of a surprise. "Okay, well I will get with Louise. I know she will let everyone know. She seems to have everybody's contact info around here. Plus some neighbors are bound to be at the funeral tomorrow morning."

"Sounds good. Y'all have a good evening." He saluted us and then bounded off the porch.

Everyone was a suspect, including my own missing daughter. I picked up Tyric, who was still knocked out to the world. Good for him. Kisha ran through the living room to the kitchen with Porgy right behind her.

I placed the tray on the counter. On my shopping list on the refrigerator, right under diapers, I marked down formula. At my age, I really shouldn't be thinking about or considering this kind of stuff on my grocery list. Funny, when I had Junior, I had to physically wash diapers. By the time Cedric came along, I had started using disposable diapers. The diapers these days were expensive and had so many fancy smancy features.

I slid my eyes across my refrigerator up to the corner. A little white card held in place by a yellow plastic banana magnet, caught my attention. She would have been the last person in the world I wanted to talk to, but it might be a good idea to invite her to the impromptu meeting too. I pulled the card down and then grabbed the phone. I waited with my heart pounding in my chest.

"This is Detective Wilkes, can I help you?"

"Yes, Detective, this is Eugeena Patterson."

"Mrs. Patterson. Good to hear from you. I was about to contact you."

It figured. I didn't have who she wanted, but I was going to do everything I could to protect my daughter.

130

20

The twins eyed me, but at least this time neither Annie Mae or Willie Mae assaulted me with questions. With Kisha holding tight to my hand, and behind me, Cedric holding little Tyric, we walked up toward the front of the church sanctuary. I knew Amos was behind us. He mentioned wanting to stay in the back of the church to observe. I'm glad Cedric pulled some time off to come this morning. It meant a lot. I felt okay, but with so much was on my mind, I had difficulty picking my feet up to walk.

As we drew closer, I focused on the beautiful baby blue casket. I was trying to process that Mary's body was in there. An empty shell of a woman I would sorely miss.

"Psst, Eugeena." I pulled my eyes from the casket. Cora waved me over to where she had saved seats. Cedric, the children and I squeezed into the third row. I hugged Cora. She clutched my hand as I sat down. With her on one side and my son on the other, my uneasiness wasn't quite so over-whelming.

This church was where Mary and I really met. Later, we learned we lived in the same neighborhood. Not too long after that Mary made the transition from working at the high school down to the middle school. We sat in each other's classrooms talking about our students, the curriculum and our families.

"Grandma."

I looked down and Kisha. "Yes, honey."

"What's that?"

It didn't occur to me until now that Kisha had never been to a funeral. The four year old had sense enough to know this wasn't like a regular church service. "Someone special is in there. She's sleeping right now. God decided to take her home with him."

"Why?"

"God wanted her home. She has people waiting for her in heaven. Don't worry, she's happy."

All this time I thought of all my regrets. It certainly wasn't pleasant the way Mary died, but she was with her Jennifer again. Her precious Jimmy too. Tears sprung to my eyes.

"So, why do they have the box? Is she okay in there?"

"Honey, her body is in there, but she's with God in heaven. We'll talk more later."

Pastor Jones rose, "Church, we come to lay to rest our dear sister Mary Fleming. This is not an occasion to be sad, but one to rejoice in her homegoing. Some of us have loved ones on the other side. So, we rejoice because Sister Fleming is with her Creator and loved ones."

As Pastor Jones continued, I felt a little hand come up near my face.

Kisha peered into my eyes. "Grandma, you crying?"

I touched my face; sure enough it was wet.

The choir stood and sang "Precious Lord." I looked down at the program and almost had an inclination to run out of the church. My name was on the program.

Lord, what do I say? What do I say when I was the one who found her? My daughter is wanted for questioning.

Mary reached out to my daughter before she reached out to me. What did that say about me? In all my self-righteousness had I built my own wall so high, Mary wasn't willing to try to climb?

Before I knew it, Cedric prodded me from the side and looked with concern. I nodded I was okay. It was time to say something.

Lord, don't let my legs fail me.

I grabbed the microphone from the side podium and looked at the audience. Not sure why, but I saw Amos' face first despite him being in the back. His eyes were warm and supportive. I smiled back at him.

"Church, thank you for coming. I'm not really sure what to say."

My eyes swung around the church, noting most of the pews were filled.

"Mary was a kind, sweet person. She and I became friends years ago. I can't say we kept in touch as much, but I always still enjoyed seeing her smile. She was one of those people when she smiled it truly lit up her eyes. And ..."

I caught sight of Carmen. I wasn't sure why she was there. She didn't really know Mary. Did she?

"Like pastor said. She loved her family. She is probably ecstatic to be with her husband and daughter." I choked on the word daughter, not knowing where mine was located. "We should rejoice with her."

My eyes fell back on Amos. Something about that man stabilized me. All the years I was married to Ralph, despite our struggles, he was my rock. Not the Rock of Ages, mind you, but someone God sent to be by my side and me by his.

"You know, I think sometimes we get caught up in people being just like us. Mary was always herself. She willingly became a vessel God could use. No matter what she went through, she kept her heart open, willing to love anyone who let her. The church will miss her spirit. I will too."

As I sat, Cedric handed Tyric over to me. I noticed he gazed across the pews. I turned to catch Carmen staring back. When she saw me looking, she turned her head back to the choir.

I curled the baby in my arms and looked over at Cedric who had also turned his head to the choir. What was that about?

After the eulogy, Cedric took the children back to the house. Neither of them needed to be out in the heat and I couldn't take any more of Kisha's questions. Not then.

As Cora and I walked through the cemetery gates, she had hooked her arm into mine. I was grateful for the support. Across the cemetery plot I caught sight of Amos. He seemed to be in deep conversation with... Detective Wilkes.

Before Cora and I had walked three yards, Amos and Detective Wilkes were on the move. In my direction. Amos nodded when he walked up and planted himself next to me. I peered into his eyes. He turned away and looked into the crowd. Detective Wilkes cleared her throat and glanced over at Cora.

"Mrs. Patterson, do you mind if we talk to you? Alone."

"I'm family. Whatever you have to say to Eugeena, you can say to me." Cora crossed her arms.

With that we followed Detective Wilkes. Amos was strangely solemn next to me. Once we were a good bit away from the burial plot, Detective Wilkes stopped. "Mrs. Patterson, I understand you reported your daughter missing in Richland County on Tuesday."

I looked at Amos, who seemed to be studying a tombstone. I hoped to find Leesa before this woman did. "Yes, I went to her apartment Tuesday. I talked to a neighbor and thought it might be a good idea to get some help."

The woman frowned, "Mrs. Patterson, you could have told me on Sunday."

"It wasn't twenty-four hours yet." I lowered my voice, so not to attract attention from the funeral attendees. "Plus, you came into my home telling me my daughter was a suspect."

"Not a suspect. Just a person of interest." The detective pointed to the open grave where Pastor Jones stood talking under the tent. "She might have been the last person to see Mrs. Fleming alive. With Mrs. Fleming being somewhat of a recluse it's been hard to piece together the woman's activities leading up to her death."

The detective did have a point. "Detective, I can't believe my daughter ..."

"Eugeena." Amos took hold of my elbow.

The gesture stopped me cold. Why did these two pull me to the side at the cemetery? My shoulders sank. I'm not sure I wanted to know. "You have something to tell me."

Redness creeped around Detective Wilkes' freckled face. I'm sure it was more than heat-related. "Yes, Mrs. Patterson. I received a call from the Richland County Sheriff. Does your daughter drive an aqua blue Nissan Altima?"

I slapped my hand to my mouth. All I could do was nod.

Amos' hand moved from my elbow to draping his arm around my shoulder. "Now don't panic, Eugeena. They found her car, but not Leesa."

My hand shook now. I gasped, "What does that mean?"

Amos quietly said, "She still out there."

21

Amos wanted to drive me back home since Cedric left earlier with the children. I told him Cora would. I stared out the passenger window. I'm sure he thought I needed space, but I wanted to be mad with him. Not very reasonable, but I needed someone to be angry with. It was probably a man's fault that my daughter was out there. Some man named Chris. How is it that I didn't even know his last name? Nor what he looked like?

Then there was that slim chance Leesa was involved in Mary's death. I refused to believe she was and pounded myself inside for even considering it. I prayed to the Lord that I didn't have to attend another funeral. Ralph's been a missing hole in my life I have slowly mended, but one of my children going before me, I couldn't take the idea.

"That man really cares about you."

I turned around to face Cora. "Have you lost your mind? My daughter is Lord knows where and you trying to be a matchmaker?"

Cora slapped the steering wheel. "That's not what I'm trying to do and you know it. I'm just as worried as you are. I just wanted you to know you were a bit short with Mr. Jones."

"He'll be alright." I had every right to be huffy.

A tiny bit of regret crept in as I watched Amos pull his truck in front of my house. Cora parked behind Cedric's Lexus, which was parked in the driveway. I thought back to the night when Amos and I sat on the porch and Leesa drove up. I wished her car was in my driveway and hadn't been found on the side of some road.

As I walked toward the front porch, Amos called my name.

"Eugeena, wait a minute."

Cora cut her eye at me. "Talk to the man, he's trying to help you."

I threw my hands up and stopped to wait for Amos. "So, what happens now?"

"We are going to find her. Wilkes will circulate the photo you gave us to the television networks. Doing it now as we speak. Plus, don't forget about the meeting."

The meeting. Do I really want to have a neighborhood watch meeting with my daughter out there? "There has got to be something else I can do? She's my child."

"Stay put. Leesa might call you."

"It's been almost a week."

"Eugeena. Leave it up to the law enforcement. Wilkes told us to continue with the meeting."

I closed my eyes. "Do you really think it could be someone around here?"

"It's crucial we observe folks for any suspicious behaviors. Someone might just be cocky and think they can get off the hook especially if they were trying to lead us to looking at Leesa. Has to be someone who knows your family."

"Okay. I will prepare the best I can."

"Good. We should have a good crowd. If you need anything, call me."

Cora was sitting on the porch. "What's the plan?"

"I'm still to go on with this neighborhood watch meeting tomorrow."

Cora stood and stared at me. "How in the world did you get that assignment?"

I shook my head. "I'm still trying to figure that out." We shuffled into the house. The television was exceptionally loud in the living room. I saw why. Cedric popped off the couch. "Mama, why didn't you tell me? Leesa's photo is all over the news. They found her car."

"Yes." I looked past Cedric to the woman sitting on my couch. Seems like my son wasn't too worried about his sister. "Carmen."

She stood. "Hello, Mrs. Patterson. I'm so sorry about your daughter. Is there something we can do?"

I ignored Carmen and glared at Cedric. "Where are the kids?"

"We put them to bed as soon as we came in, they were both tired."

"What's this *we* stuff? How long have you *two* been here?"

Cora cleared her throat. "Eugeena! Why don't you sit down?" Cora moved next to me and gently led me to the chairs. "I will check on the children." I sat down hard in the recliner. Too tired to even prop my feet and stared at the television.

"Mama..." Cedric prodded.

I waved at my son like he was a mosquito. "Shhh... I need to hear what they are saying."

I heard Carmen whisper to Cedric, "I think I better go." The two walked out into the hallway while I struggled to follow the report. The photo was about four years old, but that was my Leesa for the entire world to see. I held my head down. I felt in my heart she was still okay, but where could she be? Why did she leave her car? Did somebody have her somewhere?

Cedric joined me on the couch. He rubbed his hands across his head like his dad used to do when he was upset. "Mama, what can we do? I can't believe this is happening. We should be out there looking for her."

"Cedric, can we get our hands on Tyric's birth certificate?"

Cedric blew out a breath. "You think he had something to do with her missing? Leesa probably listed his name, but I can't get my hands on that information legally."

"We need to find this Chris somebody?"

"We? You mean the police?"

I knew what I meant. There was no way I'm going to just sit here and do nothing. Lord, I pray you continue to protect my child and you might want to protect that Chris boy from

140

me. He was going to meet the grandmother of his child and it wasn't going to be pretty.

22

I've done some crazy things in my life. Banging on Amos Jones' door and inviting myself into a man's house? That was a first for me.

Amos opened the door, still dressed in his suit pants, with a white tank t-shirt. He'd manage to stay rather fit except for some thickness around the waist. Not bad looking for an older guy. "Eugeena."

"Hey, I need your help. Well, aren't you going to invite me in?"

Amos shook his head. "Come on in woman."

Standing inside his foyer, I noticed Amos' walls still had a woman's touch to them. He probably hadn't changed anything from the way his wife had decorated.

"Now what's this about, Eugeena?"

"I need to find Chris."

Amos squinted at the paper. "Chris?"

"Tyric's daddy. I believe he has something to do with Leesa disappearing."

"Well, we should leave this to the police."

"I *want* to find him."

"That's *not* a good idea."

"I have his son."

"I understand you want to do something, but you are talking a little bit crazy. We told Detective Wilkes everything. The law can locate the man faster than we can."

I huffed. "Aren't you the law?"

"I'm retired, woman."

"So? You've managed to stick your nose into the investigation of Mary's death."

"Wait a minute now. She's a neighbor. I couldn't just sit around and not do anything."

"Exactly. Which is why you can't expect me sit by and do nothing while my daughter is missing."

Amos shook his head. "What's your plan, woman?"

"We need to get back to Leesa's apartment and get in this time. I know my daughter, she probably left some clue that no one else would understand but me."

"I will go with you. We will look around. But if we find something, we tell the police, understand?"

I smiled. "Gotcha."

He pulled his shirt from the back of the chair. "I can't believe I'm doing this. I would never let a civilian get me to do something like this. Let's try not to get into any trouble."

Did he say not get into any trouble? Looks like I was in knee-deep and would dive in even further to find my daughter. I knew she was alive.

23

By the time we arrived in Columbia, the sun had gone down and the moon sat full in the sky. As we rode, I can't say my nerves improved any, but I had more appreciation for Amos than I did earlier.

"You still miss her."

"Everyday." His voice was hoarse.

"I miss Ralph. Kind of funny, it seemed like we didn't or at least he didn't like me much sometimes. After the first heart attack, he softened up a bit." I laughed. "Actually a lot."

Amos peered at me in the darkness, with one hand on the steering wheel. "I've had death at my door a few times. It makes you think about what really matters."

"You right about that."

"Eugeena, why do you think the police are trying to place Leesa at Mary's house? Would she have had a reason to be there?"

"Maybe. I found this letter Mary had written her a few weeks ago. Mary finally decided to clean out her daughter's things and she found the stolen ring."

"Ring?"

"Oh you don't know the story, do you?"

"Nope."

"At one time Mary and I, our families were tight. Our daughters hung out together, really best friends. Mary and I worked at Sugar Creek Middle School. Ralph and her husband Clarence often fished together."

"What happened? I rarely saw you two talk."

"I know. To this day I don't know what happened. I know Mary came over one day like usual and said Leesa took a family heirloom that was really special to her."

"The ring?"

"You guessed it." I rubbed my forehead. The event still felt silly to me. "Anyway, I am known to lose my temper sometimes."

"Really, I hadn't noticed."

I laughed at Amos' attempt to be sarcastic. I could see his white teeth. He was a beautiful man.

"To make a long story short, I blew up, she got mad, she told some people about what happened, I talked to some people, our daughters got mad with each other, we didn't talk for months and then..."

Amos prodded me. "Then what?"

"The accident. Jennifer had been attending a camp for honor students at Duke University and her father was bringing her home. They were hit by a drunk driver. Jimmy died instantly and Jennifer hung on for a few weeks."

"My God."

"Leesa really was affected by her best friend's death. She became a handful. There were so many times I wanted to go by and talk to Mary. Life just took over."

Soon we'd pulled up in front of the apartment. There were no lights in the windows.

"Well, we're here." Amos opened his door. "Let's see if the woman you talked to saw anything else."

The television blared from the door, but I reached over and pressed the doorbell. I hoped Mrs. Hattie's hearing was still good. I had a feeling with the voices from the television talking to us outside the woman might not come to the door.

"Who's there?"

I was wrong. This woman must be like another Louise. Always alert and being nosy. "Mrs. Hattie, it's Leesa's mother."

Locks clinked and clanked on the inside of the door. Finally, Hattie peeked between the crack in the door. She opened the door wider. "Oh, you're back." I saw her take in Amos on my side. "Brought your husband this time."

If I could turn red I would've. "No, this is a ..." Well, what was Amos? It felt silly calling him a neighbor. "... a family friend." My family barely knew Amos, but that was his title for now.

"Oh, well you know I thought I heard someone up there a few hours ago."

"You did?" Leesa could be up there right now.

"Yeah, I even banged on the ceiling. A whole lot of bumping and thumping. I could barely hear my television."

Apparently a *Law and Order* fan too, I could hear the distinct melody playing from inside. Me and the whole apartment complex. Either she'd turned it up to avoid hearing the noise upstairs or she really couldn't hear. I was itching to get upstairs. If the noise caused Hattie to turn up her television, something was awry.

"Did you see Leesa or uh ... Chris?"

"I haven't seen anybody since you came by the other day. I've been real under the weather. Some kind of stomach virus, I think."

"Thank you, Mrs. Hattie." There was no need to subject Amos and myself to TMI or too much information. Hattie lived alone and could keep us here all night. I had to find my daughter.

I huffed my way up the stairs to my chagrin. It had been several days since I exercised and I hoped Amos wouldn't notice my struggle with the stairs. By the time we got to the top, he didn't look much better than I did. I guess being retired, he'd lost some of his physical fitness.

I rang the door bell, waited a few minutes and then tried banging.

"Hold on, Eugeena. Give her a chance to get to the door if she's in there."

Yeah, if she's in there. "Leesa." I called out. "Open the door."

I felt the hair on my arms rise. While I could still hear Hattie's television from below, now muffled, it was very silent behind my daughter's apartment door.

I placed my hand on the knob.

Click.

I turned toward Amos, who looked back at me.

He placed his arm out in front of me. "Stand back."

I expected him to pull out a piece, but he didn't, he pushed me behind him and slowly turned the knob. The door swung open, showing darkness. I could see the outlines of the couch Leesa inherited when Ralph thought it was okay for us to upgrade our living room furniture. Amos stepped inside. "You stay here."

Yeah right. I moved in close behind Amos, stepping on the heel of his shoe. He spun around, ready to say something, but I put my index finger to my mouth. Now was not the time to scold me or hold a mother back from going inside her child's dark apartment.

I remembered where the light switch was on the wall. Bright light illuminated the small living room and dinette area on the side. The ceiling fan part of the light started whirring slowly and then picked up speed. The air lifted some papers that were lying on the coffee table. I walked over and peered down at the papers. Some textbooks sat on the table as well. It looked like Leesa had been studying for a class. A brief spurt of joy passed through me since I'd only been nagging her for years to take some courses at the community college.

"She's not here, Amos. Let's go. I don't know what we are going to do now."

"Well, we can still try to find this Chris fellow. Maybe she has an address written down somewhere."

"That's true. She keeps a desk in her bedroom." I headed down the narrow dark hallway, stepping on some plush toy that talked back to me. I reached down to stop the high-pitched yakking. The toy appeared to be Elmo, one of Kisha's favorites. How come Leesa didn't pack him? Had Kisha grown tired of this toy already? The more I thought about it, I realized Leesa didn't make plans to stay long.

I switched the lamp on in the room, illuminating an unmade bed. Not uncharacteristic of Leesa. Her room though more adult like, still resembled the messiness of her childhood bedroom back at Sugar Creek. I walked over to the desk, which used to be in her room when she lived at home.

I searched through the desk drawer and found what appeared to be a journal of some sort. Now I definitely wasn't one to snoop into my children's stuff, but at a time like this, I had to flip through the pages.

"Did you find something?"

I jumped and screeched.

Amos appeared sheepish. "Sorry, didn't mean to scare you."

Holding one hand over my chest, I held up the notebook. "I found this journal. I guess I'm a little nervous to be flipping through it."

Amos moved closer to me. "No time to worry about being a snoop now."

He was right. I flipped pages. They weren't dated in any consistency as most journals go. An entry from late last year grabbed my attention.

I'm pregnant. I've been in denial, but I know the feeling. I wanted to ask Mama what to do, but she might really be disappointed with me this time. I knew better. I haven't even introduced Chris to Mama yet. I'm not sure she will like him or not. I'm not even sure I want to keep this baby.

I sucked in my teeth. I had no idea what turmoil Leesa went through to have Tyric. I continued to another page, dated two months ago.

Mama keeps calling me. I try to hurry her off the phone. She would never admit it, but I know that has to hurt her feelings. I keep thinking why am I keeping this pregnancy a secret. She's going to find out. That's if I live long enough. Chris is crazy. He hit Kisha today and I just lurched at him. He knocked me back. I would've hit the floor if I hadn't caught the counter. I told him I'm pregnant. Are you crazy?

My heart did flip-flops. I looked up at Amos, who was studying me. "We definitely need to find this Chris. He seems to be a scary man." I peered back down to go to the next entry, but that's when a click came from up front. Amos and I eyed each other.

"Leesa."

"Wait, Eugeena."

I was already gone, halfway towards the living room, ready to take my child in my arms and take her back home with me. I would not let any harm come to her.

The door opened.

I stopped, my heart pounding in my chest.

It wasn't Leesa.

24

A man stepped through the door. His presence threw me off as I took in his attire. He was at least six foot three or four, ebony black skin and underneath his blue uniform, he certainly wasn't slim. Muscular, kind of built like a football player. Really the man was huge.

I felt Amos' presence behind me and for the tenth time in a week I was glad to have him with me, although between Amos and me we still might not be able to take the man down. I mean, was he really a cop? I mustered up some confidence to ask, "Excuse me officer, why are you here? Do you have some identification on you?"

The man took off his hat displaying a head bare around the sides, with only a low tuft of hair going down the middle. He must have been a Marine or a part of the military at one time. "Ma'am, I can ask you the same question since I had a report of a break-in?"

"Break-in. Oh no." I whirled to Amos and then back. "No wait, you're mistaken. This is my daughter's apartment. She's missing. You know this already. They should have alerts all over where you work."

"Yes, they have circulated some information about a young woman."

"Well, do you have anything new? Like who is this Chris guy?"

The man's eyes narrowed. Amos moved up beside me.

It took a moment before the cop answered. Almost like he wanted to arrest me or hit me. But for what?

"I'm Chris. Chris Black."

They have a cliché saying. You could have heard a pin drop. In the silence that followed Chris Black revealing himself, I didn't know whether to drop to the floor or drop kick him.

I finally found my voice. "You are my daughter's boyfriend." A cop. The one meant to protect. My daughter seemed to be on the run because of him. "Where is she?" Amos reached for my arm, but I didn't care.

As I lurched forward, Chris stepped back and held up his hands. "Ma'am, I don't want to have to haul you in for assaulting an officer. You might want to calm down."

"And you might want to tell me where my daughter is Officer Chris Black." I ain't one to go toe to toe with the law, but I'd managed to stand less than seven inches from Chris, who I might add, stood a foot taller than me.

"Mrs. Patterson, I don't know Leesa's whereabouts."

"That is the wrong answer. What are you really doing here then? Nobody called in a break-in did they?"

"Mrs. Hattie reported hearing noise upstairs. I was in the vicinity when the call came in on the radio."

I caught myself. My hands were balled in a fist. Lord, me and you going to have to have a talk. Just when I think I have my temper down, I get a curve ball thrown at me. I stepped back. "You might be right about that. I still like to know what kind of person you must be that my daughter never introduced you to me."

"Maybe you two didn't have the best relationship."

Oh no he didn't? My hands flexed into fists again. "Maybe you weren't the man she thought Mama would like."

"Okay, that's enough. Eugeena, and ahem, Officer Black." Amos placed his hand in front of me coaxing me backward. "Time is crucial and we need to try to locate Leesa. I think we are all aware there are some children involved here."

My grandchildren. Amos was right. We needed to find Leesa.

Amos continued, "Can you tell us the last time you saw her?"

"Two months ago."

"What?" Amos strained to hold me back. "You trying to tell me, my daughter had your child and you have not been by to see her or your son?"

Chris bit his lip. "It's not because I didn't want to. She wouldn't let me."

I looked at what appeared to be some wetness formed around Chris' eyes. There is no way I'm going to fall for that. Eugeena Patterson knew when she was being manipulated. What Mr. Black didn't know is Hattie already told me he'd been by harassing my daughter.

153

He'd better not have laid a hand on her. If he did, it would take a whole lot of Jesus in me not to lay Chris Black out. For good.

25

I wasn't satisfied until Amos called and I talked on the phone with Detective Wilkes. This morning I called her again and she assured me she would contact Chris' captain to get an official statement. Two months. I'm sure being a cop with access to all kinds of venues; he could have cornered Leesa anytime he wanted to. At least one mystery was solved. Until my daughter appeared, I had to still clear her name of a being a possible murder suspect.

If what Amos said was true, I could be entertaining the real suspect in my own living room this evening.

To provide me a bit of a reprieve, Cora was kind enough to take the kids over to her home for the night. I almost wish they were still here. Why is it folks drive you crazy when they are around and you miss them when they are gone?

Porgy started barking as if he protested the thought.

"What's wrong with you, dog? Shush."

The front doorbell rang. Wow, I'm impressed. Porgy might make a decent guard dog. He needed to pull his weight around here.

I looked at the clock. I had at least thirty minutes before folks started showing up for the meeting. "Who is it?" The peephole showed nobody at the door. I stood for a second. I looked at Porgy. His body was erect and poised. Somebody was out there.

The doorbell pierced my ears again. My good ear too. This time through the peephole I recognized the face. I opened the door.

Tamara bit her lip and shrugged her shoulders. "I know I'm early, but I thought maybe you could use some help."

"That's sweet of you. Come on in. I'm certainly not about to turn down the help, honey." Tamara followed me to the kitchen. Or tried. Porgy sniffed her heals and growled. "Porgy, what's your problem. I'm going to have to put you up. You can't aggravate my guests."

"Oh you don't need to do that."

I looked at Tamara to see if she meant it, but she seemed to be a little paralyzed by the dog. "I tell you what, I started some sandwiches on the table in there, why don't you start slicing them and I will put him upstairs." Back downstairs, I entered the kitchen. "Wow, you are good with that slicing for somebody not in the kitchen much."

Tamara laughed lightly. "Uhm Miss Eugeena, what are we discussing tonight at the meeting? Did the cops find out anything new?"

"That's a good question. I did invite Detective Wilkes, so maybe she will have some things to share with us."

"You were friends with Mrs. Fleming, right?"

I'm not sure how much I wanted to go into the past with Tamara. "We were closer in the past."

Tamara frowned. "Did you grow apart?"

"Something like that. Can you pass me the oven mittens off the table?"

I turned my back and pulled out the oven fried chicken. The recipe was getting better and better all the time. I still missed deep frying the chicken, but I couldn't risk cooking in my old style. Lord knows, my grandmama and mama passed on some good eats, just not good methods. Of course back then black folks had to cook their food the best way they could. No excuses today.

The door bell rang.

"Tamara, can you answer the door. Just sit the guests in the living room. If you need more chairs, there are some fold-up ones in the hall closet."

"Not a problem."

I took the vegetable tray and dip and placed it on the side table.

"Hey Eugeena, I bought some green bean casserole. How are you?"

"Here are some sodas. Heard about your daughter. We are praying."

"Got potato salad."

I smiled. Smiled and thanked neighbor after neighbor as they sat various goodies on the table. I didn't realize how many people knew Leesa.

Tamara saddled up beside me. "Wow, look at this table. I feel bad I didn't bring anything." She lowered her voice. "Are you okay? I heard about your daughter. Should you even do this meeting tonight?"

I reached over and hugged the young woman. "I'm fine. Everything is going to be fine."

I'm not sure if I was trying to convince me or Tamara. I hugged her again."Why don't you find a seat?" I clasped my hands together and watched her sit in the corner of the couch. At the other end of the couch was Wayne.

We locked eyes. He broke out in a familiar smile; a hint of the young boy I used to know appeared.

Maybe I had been too judgmental of Wayne. God took people as they were, I needed to do the same. Still I couldn't deny my delight about Wayne cleaning up. Last time, he was looking awfully scruffy on my furniture.

I scanned the other neighbors' faces. Many folks were here for the first time. Other faces had showed up for a second round of the meeting. The doorbell rang again. Tamara started to rise, but I held my hand. I'm glad I answered the door myself.

"Amos, right on time."

He wore black slacks and a red polo shirt. Why did this man look like he was heading to the golf course all the time? I needed to ask him what his handicap was.

Like I knew a thing about golf.

"Our guest of honor is here too." Amos stepped to the side.

Detective Wilkes was in rare form tonight. Her usually frayed hair was hanging down around her shoulders. Child even brushed her red locks. Was that a little bit of lip gloss on her lips? "Good to see you, Detective. You look nice tonight."

"Thanks for the invite. This is a good idea you and Mr. Jones hatched up here." Once inside, Detective Wilkes' green eyes scoped the room. "This is a good crowd. How are you holding up?"

"As well as I can. Thanks for asking. Anything out of Chris?"

"He's sticking to his story about not seeing your daughter. I have a couple of colleagues checking out his activities over the last week or so. Don't worry; we will nail him if he's done anything unusual."

"I hope so. Well, I guess I should get the meeting started soon."

Wait a minute. Where was Louise? She should have been here first thing.

I tugged on Amos' shirt sleeve. "Have you seen Louise?"

"No, I thought she'd be here already. That woman would have made a fine spy."

"Mmmm. I wonder if her hip is bothering her again. She didn't call. I'm going to head next door to check on her."

"Sure, thing I'll think that spread of food you got over there will keep folks busy. Is that fried chicken I smell?"

I knew it. He was a fried chicken man. "I hope you like it. It's a little different."

As I walked across my yard, I really did hope he liked it. A way to a man's heart was through his stomach. Without Amos' help, I wouldn't have been able to get through this week.

"Ughhh." Something plowed into me so hard; I stumbled backwards to the ground.

"Miss Eugeena, I'm sorry. I'm so sorry."

The sun was low, showing pink overtones in the sky. I gazed up into Carmen's face. I didn't know if it was the sky behind her, but the girl looked a hot mess. "Carmen?"

"I'm sorry, let me help you up."

I grabbed the woman's hand. She yanked me up, which surprised me more than my bruised rear end. "You sure don't know your strength, girl."

"I didn't want to be late for the meeting." She bent down and picked up a long rectangular object. "I hope the brownies are okay. I almost forgot about them and ..."

I patted her on the arm. "I'm sure they're fine and thanks for going through the trouble. Just slow down, okay?"

"Yes, ma'am."

I peered into the girl's eyes. The outside light was playing tricks on me, but the rims of her eyes appeared to be red. Never mind her and my son was hanging out on my couch yesterday after the funeral. "You had a late night at the hospital?"

She looked away. "Something like that. I better get inside. Are you coming?"

"I'm heading to fetch Louise. I'll be in there soon. Just sit your brownies on the table with the rest of the food."

I watched the woman who with all her height seemed to be almost like a little girl lost tonight. Between her and Tamara, it seemed like I was doing more mothering to them than my own daughter. I sure hope Cedric didn't have anything to do with what appeared to be recent tears.

Louise's front windows were awfully dark. Knowing the night owl the woman tended to be, that definitely was odd. It was also very quiet. Louise loved watching game shows and this time of day she would being switching from *Jeopardy* and back to *Who Wants to Be a Millionaire*. I told her once she needed to be a contestant on one of the shows before the good Lord took her home.

I rang the door bell. Surely, she didn't take out her hearing aid. Knowing Louise had to hear everything, her silence wasn't sitting well with my stomach. I went over to the swing set on her porch and reached around the back of the chair. Sure enough the spare key was still there. Years ago we worked out a system for each other to get into each other's homes if we had to help each other out.

This seemed like one of those times. Now I was a fairly intelligent woman. I should have returned to my house for Amos or Detective Wilkes, but with several neighbors in my home, it might not be good to alert them to anything. Not yet. Louise could be knocked out sleeping for all I know.

The door clicked and swung open. Once inside, I closed the door. "Louise." My voice bounced off the walls. I turned my head towards the living room which was pitch black. Not a single lamp on.

Maybe I need to get Amos.

Instead I kept walking down a hallway. Since Louise's hip had grown increasingly frail, she'd converted what used to be a guest bedroom to her bedroom. I walked up to the closed door and I knocked. Then, I reached for the knob, the metal felt cool to my skin. With one movement, I turned the knob and flung the door open.

If Louise was asleep, the sound of the door banging against the dresser should have given her a heart attack. My own heart seemed to have changed positions in my chest, practically beating near my throat. The lamp on the nightstand showed a made bed. Just as I thought. The woman never slept.

I peered down the hallway. The kitchen door was closed. Louise usually kept the door propped open like I did.

My head felt woozy all of a sudden. Too much blood flow. *Have I eaten today?* I spent most of the day walking the floor and the other half cooking food, still walking the floor in a way.

Maybe I needed to get Amos.

I chanted. *I need to get Amos. I need to get Amos.*

I hadn't convinced myself very well to stop what I was about to do. I pushed the kitchen door open slowly, peering through the sliver. The light above the double porcelain sink illuminated the kitchen. I opened the door wider. A jar of honey sat unopened on the table, Louise loved honey in her tea. I looked at the counter. Two coffee cups. On the stove, the silver tea pot glistened.

My eyes traveled from the stove to the floor. That's when I saw them.

Those ugly green clogs Louise loved. I knew they were probably comfortable, but I didn't agree that comfort had to look like something an ogre would wear.

The clogs weren't flat on the floor though, but sticking straight up to the sky.

I shuffled to the counter and then around. Images swarmed before my eyes.

Oh my friend. No, no, no.

26

Was this a dream? I opened my eyes, and then shut them tight. The light stung my eyes producing tears. I pried them open again and blinked. My surroundings were familiar, but this was not my house. I tried to sit up, but strong arms held me back.

"Whoa, Eugeena keep it steady?"

I opened my eyes wider and turned to the left. "Amos?"

"I was worried. Boy, am I glad I went looking for you."

That's when I remembered. I wasn't in my house, but Louise's. And the last thing I saw was Louise's body laid out on the floor. "Is she..."

"She's still breathing. It appeared she smacked her head pretty hard. Kind of strange with her being in the kitchen like..." Amos stopped and peered at me, the whole time he had been rubbing his bald head.

He didn't have to say it out loud. I was already thinking it. I was also thinking was I next? Mary, Louise and I all lived on the same side of the street. "I thought she was dead. I knew something wasn't right as soon as I stepped in the door."

"Why didn't you come get me, Eugeena? The person could have still been in the house?"

Or just left. Things fell back into place as my head cleared.

"You know before I arrived, I ran into Carmen."

Amos raised an eyebrow, "What do you mean you ran into her?"

"The girl just about bowled me over. I don't know if she was just running to get to my house on time or if she was running from something."

"She did appear a little out of sorts when she arrived at your house. You're not thinking she assaulted Louise. What for?"

"I have no idea, but she and Wayne have been pretty tight. Louise noticed them together all the time. The woman isn't the most discreet sometimes, she might have seen something and they saw her."

"Well, I'm sure it's nothing. I can tell you Wayne is getting his life together. I helped him get a J-O-B. All the boy needed was something to do. When Louise wakes up, she will tell us for sure. In the meantime, we need to get you checked out."

"For what? I'm fine." I lifted my body from the floor, but I felt like Peter must have felt when he realized he was walking on water. Except my foot didn't like the idea of walking at all. "I think I better lay back down."

Amos steadied me with his hands around my waist. For a minute there, I was surprised his arms fit around me.

Am I feverish?

A voice came from around Amos. "She needs to eat something."

I looked around Amos to see Carmen standing with crackers in her hand.

"Here you might want to have something to eat to help jumpstart your blood glucose."

Spoken like a true doctor except I wasn't too sure whether or not Carmen had tried to take a life instead of save one. Was she really running to my house with the tray of brownies or running from a crime scene?

Amos nodded. "Good idea, Carmen. Eugeena, you should eat something."

Carmen handed the package of crackers to Amos, who then passed them to me. Carmen cleared her throat and said, "I hope you don't mind, but I called Dr. Patterson. He wants us to get you down to the hospital."

I pushed a cracker into my mouth. They tasted like paper, but I ate until Amos was satisfied. Earlier in the evening, someone paid a visit to Louise. I simply wasn't buying she just fell and bumped her head. There were two tea cups on the counter. Knowing Louise, she spoke her mind without thinking. Had she uncovered the real murderer? If she did, she practically got herself killed.

We arrived at the hospital in what seemed like no time. Cedric met us in the emergency room. "Mama, how are you feeling?"

"I'm better. The shock got to me, but right now I really want to see Louise."

"In a little while. From what I hear she's still unconscious, plus she has cops waiting to speak to her, so you might be standing in line."

Detective Wilkes was at the neighborhood watch. She had to have noticed another person had been in the kitchen too. "Amos, did Detective Wilkes have anything to say about the meeting?"

Amos looked over at Cedric, then back to me. "She didn't mention anything new, but she was a little concerned that you found two people who were obviously assaulted."

"What do you mean she was concerned? I can't help it if I have a special concern for people. I knew something wasn't right with Mary and then again with Louise?"

"Calm down, Mama. She is probably just concerned about your safety. You might want to plan to spend the night at my place."

"I can't do that, Cedric. Cora will be bringing the kids back in the morning. Take me to see Louise please."

We made it up to the sixth floor where Louise was in intensive care. It took some talking, but the nurse let me see Louise because she didn't have any family. I was her next door neighbor and I would have to do as kin. We all related to one another in our bloodlines.

Louise's appearance brought tears to my eyes. An ugly purple bruise peeked out from under the white bandages around the right side of her face. The top of her head was completely wrapped in bandages. The one good thing, she appeared to be breathing on her own. No tubes were attached.

I touched her hand, weathered with dark spots. Maybe she would recognize my voice and awaken.

"Louise."

I believe my friend had some of the answers I sought, but Louise's eyes remained tightly closed. I wasn't going to find out until she awakened.

I wrapped my hand around Louise's. "Sleep my friend. Get your rest. We still have to save our neighborhood."

I walked back into the hall. As I turned the corner, I could hear a loud voice coming from the right. It was distinctly deep and kind of familiar.

"Where is she? Where is my mother?"

"Calm down, sir. This is intensive care. We need you to be calm. Tell me her name."

"Louise Hopkins."

I examined the man's side profile. Well, I'll be. When did he get back into town?

"William, is that you?"

The man turned. I gawked at Louise's son. This was the boy she doted on. Her pride and joy. Now older, his hair was balding on the top and what hair he had left hung down his back in a ratty ponytail. "Eugeena. Where is she?"

Detective Wilkes walked up beside me. "Sir, are you kin to Mrs. Hopkins?"

William's face turned into an ugly snarl. "Yeah, who are you?"

The detective held out her hand. "I'm Detective Wilkes. I'm looking into your mother's case, to see if it relates to Mary Fleming."

"Mary? What does she have to do with my mother?"

I decided to break in. "Somebody killed her. Your mother was very lucky this evening. Being *alone*." Didn't Louise say her son was out shooting a documentary in the Amazon or something? She certainly didn't mention he was coming to visit. Anytime William was in town Louise made a big hoopla for him. She hadn't mentioned him in days; maybe weeks come to think about it.

William rubbed his hand across his shiny reddish forehead. "Mary's dead?" He groaned and shook his head, "I've been trying to get mother to move out of that neighborhood for years."

I cocked my eyebrow. "Louise is a staple in Sugar Creek. She knows everything and everyone. This is *her* home."

William shook his finger in my face. "Well, after we get through this ordeal, there's a new assisted living home I've been checking out."

I protested. "Your mother is independent and healthy as a horse."

He shot back at me. "Well, someone practically tried to kill her and you said someone already died. You might not think much of me, but I will protect my mother."

Could I blame him? I shifted my eyes to my own son. The concern in Cedric's eyes reflected what I saw in William's. My vulnerability level had escalated sky high.

One friend was buried yesterday. Another friend lay in a hospital bed. My daughter? I had no idea where she could be. Two young children. A little dog. I don't think I ever felt more helpless in my life. So much for organizing a neighborhood association, I couldn't keep a handle on my life. God said he wouldn't give you more than you could bear.

Hello Lord! Can you see a sistah's white flag waving in the air?

27

Cedric protested, but Amos insisted on bringing me home from the hospital. It made sense to me. Amos did live next door.

When I stepped out of the truck, I assured Amos I would be fine.

Amos nodded in my direction and said, "If you need anything, just holler."

A moan escaped my mouth when I closed the front door. I leaned against the door for a few minutes. Cora had the children, so the normal silence of the house greeted me. Well, almost. I could hear barking in the distance. I sighed again. I was getting a bit used to having a dog, but I'd been on the go so much and the dog had needs.

I retrieved Porgy and then opened the back door. My eyes watched for any signs of movement in the darkness while, Porgy ran circles and finally stopped to take care of his business.

Back inside, I added water to the tea kettle, thinking of the two mugs that were on Louise's counter. *Who came to visit Louise tonight and why?* I placed a bag of chamomile tea in my mug and eased my way into the kitchen chair, waiting for the water to boil. Porgy sat, his black button eyes watched me. I didn't know much about dogs, but he probably needed to be groomed. "I know you miss your other mama. I do too."

Missed Mary. Concerned about Louise. Worried about Leesa.

The tea kettle whistled and I poured the hot water into my mug. I sat down and took one sip, and then I stared at the kitchen chair on the other side of the table. Leesa sat in that chair almost a week ago holding Tyric in her arms.

I put my chin in my hands, elbows on the table. Tears flowed down my face. "God, I need a miracle right now. I don't know what to do. There's no way Leesa had anything to do with Mary's death or Louise's assault. Where is my daughter?" My shoulders heaved. I grabbed a napkin from the table and wiped my eyes.

Porgy whined.

"I'm okay little fellow. I'm having a bit of a pity party. I don't like when things get out of control. I like it when life is lined up and everything is flowing."

Trust me.

"What?" I looked down at Porgy. He looked back at me. I declare the dog cocked his bushy eyebrow at me as though he was saying, "Are you alright, lady?" I didn't know if I was or not, but I definitely heard a voice. Or did I? I needed to go to sleep. But how could I? All I could think about was finding more places where Leesa could be.

Trust in the Lord.

I crushed the napkin in my hand and sat very still. I was reminded of a story. Samuel. The little boy who God called out in the middle of the night while he slept. What did that old priest say to him? God's talking, sit and listen.

So I listened.

Trust in the Lord with all your heart and lean not on your own understanding.

How many years had I referred this verse to others? The rest of the scripture stated "In all your ways acknowledge him and he will make your paths straight."

I'm a fixer. Or at least I try to. Some things you can't fix on your own. Like my marriage. God intervened. I remember when I went to Ralph with the news that I was pregnant. So many girls around me moaned and groaned about how their boyfriends left them high and dry. Ralph did the right thing. Reluctantly, but he did the right thing.

I will trust the Lord.

My mother raised me and my siblings by herself, supporting us through her work in people's houses. She was the one who told me, even after I became pregnant with Junior, I would go to school and become a teacher. Something she always wanted to do.

God made a way. *I will trust the Lord.*

Then there was my Leesa. My baby girl after fifteen years of marriage. So like Ralph and so like me. God certainly kept us connected when we were often so disconnected.

I wanted to fix my relationship with Mary, but it seemed life crashed into us tossing us farther and farther away. But I can't honestly say I went to the Lord to patch up the friendship.

"Okay Lord, I hear you. I will trust you. I trust that you know where Leesa is and that you will bring her home safe."

It was after midnight, my eyes were drowsy. Porgy and I trotted up the stairs. I would start the morning off ready to locate my daughter.

While I didn't care for him to be on the bed, the dog curled up at the end of the bed around my feet. I was too exhausted to move him. I needed to rest.

I don't know how long my eyes had been closed, but I jolted awake. Porgy heard whatever I heard and stood on the bed with his nose pointed towards the door. Then he started to jump and bark.

Was it my imagination or was someone downstairs? Did Cedric come by the house anyway?

I reached for the steel baseball bat underneath the bed. I didn't believe in keeping firearms in the house so I hoped the Lord would make this bat enough of a weapon. *Lord, you said trust you. Send your angels.*

I crept towards the bedroom door. "Shhh." Porgy ran around like a maniac. I placed my ear against the door, but couldn't hear anything.

I wonder if I should call Amos. The man did say call him anytime I needed. I'm not so sure if I cared to be awakened at ... I peered at my digital clock. It read 3:00 a.m.

A crash from downstairs almost sent me to the bathroom. On myself.

I yanked the door open and sprinted into the hall. Porgy shot out in front of me heading for the stairs. Whoever was down there was about to be assaulted by an old woman and a toy dog.

With the bat in front of me, I called out, "Who's there?" as I padded down the stairs.

I realized too late that I had left my glasses on the nightstand. All I could make out was a shadow by the picture window in the living room. Porgy growled and charged further into the room.

At the bottom of the stairs, I reached my hand and felt for the hall light switch. Light illuminated the hall and part of the living room.

My intruder faced me.

28

My intruder appeared a tad bit bedraggled, but I no longer felt threatened. Porgy stopped running around and sat at my feet matching the quizzical look probably on my face. I placed the bat in the air.

"Leesa Patterson, you got some explaining to do. Do you know I could have took you out with this thing?!"

Leesa smiled, "Nice protection, Mama." Her eyes didn't match that smile.

I couldn't wait to hear this explanation, but right now my soul was overjoyed. I dropped the bat and raced over, embracing my long lost daughter. She'd only been gone a week. Felt like months. She was finally home.

"Thank you, Lord. Thank you."

An hour later, I had grabbed turkey bacon, eggs, and cheese from the fridge. Before I grilled Leesa I wanted her nourished. Bacon sizzled and I had whipped the eggs until they were nice and fluffy by the time Leesa arrived in the kitchen. Never too early for breakfast.

"Mama, you shouldn't have cooked. I'm not hungry. And it's four in the morning."

"Well, you better find some appetite somewhere because I can't eat this by myself."

Leesa sighed and sank into the kitchen chair. I turned the pan off and lifted the bacon slices onto a paper towel. I threw the dish towel around my shoulder. "Well, start explaining. What brought you back? And why you come sneaking in my house like some burglar?"

"I didn't sneak in. I have a key."

"I thought something happened to you."

Leesa eyes filled with tears. "I'm sorry. I didn't plan for all this to happen. I saw my face on the eleven-o-clock news. It occurred to me it was time to come back."

"So, last Saturday you had every intentions of dropping off the kids. Oh and by the way, one of them, practically a newborn and unknown to me until seven days ago. Then, you high-tailed it to wherever. Did it not occur to you to ask me instead of assuming I would take care of your children?"

"It's not like what it seemed."

I sat down and stared at my daughter, the breakfast in progress forgotten about. "Tell me. Make me understand, Leesa. Does this have something to do with that Chris boy?"

My daughter's eyes grew wide. "What do you know about him?"

"I met him. Thursday night at your apartment. Kind of an intimidating fellow, isn't he?"

"Chris isn't all that bad." Leesa kept her eyes on the table, fascinated by the plastic fruit in the center. "He was at my apartment?"

"Mrs. Hattie said he'd been looking for you persistently. Why didn't you tell me about him?"

"I mentioned him. I told you I had a boyfriend months ago. I just felt bad about ... Mama, I really didn't want to have Tyric." Leesa's face crumbled and her shoulders shook.

I moved my chair over and rubbed the back of her shoulders. "Things happen sometimes that we wished didn't." I know when I found out I was pregnant with Junior, I thought my whole world would come to an end. I could imagine what Leesa was thinking, already struggling with Kisha.

She lifted her head. "I love Chris in a way, but I don't know if I want to marry him and I wasn't planning to have his baby."

I could have went into a spiel about how she could have used protection or better yet kept her legs closed, but now wasn't the time, and I can't say I was one to talk. Though the only man I ever was with was the same one I married and had my other two children with. Life is different these days. People make choices not to marry. If there was no love in the first place, sometimes it's better not to if it's only going to lead to divorce later.

"Has Chris harmed you?"

"He can be intense, but he's a good guy."

"Are you trying to convince me or you? That's not what you said in that notebook."

"What? Mama, you read my journal. You did that when I was a teenager."

"Well, excuse me, but it seems to be the only way I can get information, because you certainly didn't provide answers."

"I don't tell you stuff sometimes because you can be so judgmental."

"What?" I nearly jumped out of the chair. "I'm your mother. I brought you into this world. I have a right to look after your best and this *doesn't* explain where you have been and why you left. You *are* a mother!"

Leesa looked down, her bottom lip trembled. She choked out, "It's not the same."

I sat back. "Baby girl, what's not the same?"

Leesa wailed. "I don't care for Tyric like Kisha. I mean he's my baby, but I have a hard time with him. He cries more than she did. I want to shake him so bad sometimes. He's just different. And something about me is different when I'm with him."

"Oh, Leesa." I stood and went to hug my daughter. Tight. "Why didn't you tell me? Why didn't you let me help you?"

Leesa trembled and took a long deep sigh. "I don't know what I was thinking. I couldn't handle not wanting to be pregnant, then having this baby and then ... disappointing you."

I sat in the chair beside Leesa and held her hand. We sat in silence for a long time. I tried to process all that Leesa told me and knew I needed to get her some help.

Leesa broke the silence. "Did they already have Mary's funeral?"

"Yes, it was Thursday. The same day they found your car by the side of the road. What was that about?"

Leesa shrugged. "I ran out of gas. If they checked the needle they would have saw it was on 'E.'"

Well, what could I say to that?

"You know. I went to Mary's house."

I held my breath. "When?"

"Last Friday afternoon. I guess that's why it shocked me when you said she had died. She'd sent me a letter about finding the ring. You know *the ring* that started it all."

I had to chuckle. "Where is the ring?"

"I pawned it."

"So, that explains the money in the bag? What exactly were you planning to do with the money? A diaper bag isn't exactly secure. Don't you still have the bank account we set up when you were in high school?"

"I wasn't sure what to do with it. I was so shocked that I received so much money from pawning it. Sometimes I feel like I need to make a fresh start. You know put some space between Chris and me."

Something about her strained relationship with Chris still made me uneasy. I frowned, "I thought you said he was a good guy. By the way, why aren't you letting the man see his son?"

Leesa gulped. "Let's not talk about Chris anymore. Anyway, I need to tell you about my visit with Mary. She was older, still pretty. We talked about Jenny a little. I told her it would be great to get you two talking again."

My cheeks burned. "You did?" My daughter had more courage than I did to mend past wounds. "You didn't notice anyone or anything unusual around the house?"

"I noticed Mary watching the clock. Maybe someone else was coming for a visit. Are they still looking for a suspect?"

Detective Wilkes heeded my pleas about not mentioning in the news that Leesa was wanted as a person of interest in Mary's case. "Yes. There was a witness that saw someone near the house."

"Really? Who?"

"Someone reported seeing a woman with an aqua blue Nissan."

"What?" Leesa lurched in her seat. "The police think I'm a suspect."

"Just a person of interest. You probably were the last person to see Mary alive. At least besides whoever came to see her after you left. Why didn't you come by the house?"

"I did come by the house, but you were out. That man next door, I know he saw me."

My ears perked up. "What man next door?"

Leesa pointed to the side of the house. "Over there?" He was out mowing his lawn or something.

"Amos?"

"I don't know his name. He's an old guy, probably dad's age, but he looks nice for his age."

He looked nice alright, but there were some things about Amos I apparently didn't know. Or rather he chose not to tell me. Was he the one who told the police he saw my daughter at Mary's house? Because of him my daughter was fingered as a suspect.

Oh, I wasn't too happy about that at all.

29

Seems like my daughter wasn't the only one who had some explaining to do. I invited Amos Jones over for breakfast. For the second time in about six hours, I made breakfast. This time I added a pot of grits. Then I prayed.

Lord, I trust you. I don't trust me.

The doorbell rang.

I shuffled out of the kitchen towards the front of the house. Amos smiled, not wearing a hat on his bald head today. His mouth seemed to curve up closer to his ears even more than normal.

"Good morning, Amos."

"Well, morning to you, Eugeena. I hope you slept well."

"Oh I slept better than I could have imagined." I truly did.

Amos followed me to the kitchen. The table was set real nice with my best plates. I don't often use them, but this morning charm was called for so I could get to the bottom of some things.

"Grits," I asked.

"Sounds good."

I fixed his plate.

"Aren't you eating too?"

"Yes, I am." I needed to keep my mouth preoccupied from saying the wrong thing. I did have a pet peeve about talking with my mouth full. It might serve me good.

We ate in silence for awhile. Soon Leesa entered the kitchen. She went to bed, but like me I'm sure she didn't get any sleep.

Amos looked up and almost choked. "What...?"

"Oh I meant to tell you, Leesa came back home last night."

Amos looked at Leesa and back at me. "Well, it's good to see you, young lady. You had a whole lot of people looking for you."

I raised my eye at Amos, but he didn't seem to be bothered. "Yes, somebody claimed they saw you when you went to visit Mary. We need to set the record straight with Detective Wilkes."

Amos sat his fork down and crossed his hands. "That's right. Leesa, could you tell if anyone was hanging out near or coming in the direction of Mary's home?"

Leesa sat down at the table and crossed her arms. "I know Mary seemed to be expecting someone. We were talking and then all of sudden she kept looking at the clock on the wall in the living room."

"So someone else, *not* Leesa was the last person to see Mary alive." I stood, scraped my plate and started making dish water. Amos cleaned his plate and stood beside me.

He said, "Well, we need to figure out the identity of this person."

I couldn't take it anymore. I stopped the water from running and faced Amos. "Why didn't you tell me Leesa showed up at my house the night Mary died?"

Amos shrugged his shoulders. "I knew she was your daughter. I assumed you knew she was coming or she left a message."

Leesa and I looked back and forth at each other. A very logical answer that neither one of us followed. No need to let Amos know how foolish of a mother and daughter we both were.

He did add, "Besides whoever saw Leesa at Mary's house, would have had to be near Mary's house. Remember her house is up on the hill compared to ours. Either someone drove by, walked by or saw something from their house."

Amos rubbed his chin and looked off into space for a moment.

I asked, "Amos, are you okay?"

He looked at Leesa and then at me. "You know I remember you stopping by your mother's house during the afternoon."

Leesa nodded, "Yeah, it was around five-thirty because we were back on the road to Columbia around six o'clock."

I turned to Leesa. "So how is someone claiming they saw you at Mary's house that night? We need to get you to the detective so we can tell her what you told us and get your face off the news. We will head out as soon as Cora gets here with the kids."

After Cora arrived, it took us another hour or so to get through the emotional reunions to arrive at the North Charleston police station.

Detective Wilkes' face was unreadable when we arrived at the police station.

I asked, "Do I need to get my daughter a lawyer?"

The detective replied. "That won't be necessary, Mrs. Patterson."

I eyed the detective before walking away. Someone had been trying to set my daughter up. I hoped the detective recognized she had been focusing on the wrong person all this time.

So, while my daughter was being questioned as a person of interest, I kept Kisha preoccupied while I held Tyric. *Poor baby boy!* I suspect Leesa may have been suffering from a bit of postpartum with this child. Wasn't evident with Kisha, but it's possible her hormones were making her feel emotionally detached and depressed. When this was all over, I would insist Cedric direct her to some help.

I looked at my precious grandson thankful that God answered prayers. I held a child I possibly never could have met. For that I was grateful. I always prayed for my children to be granted wisdom. Even when they didn't always understand, I hoped that they would be motivated to do the right thing.

Tyric's big brown eyes sparkled and he gurgled. He was a happy little thing. Going to be a big boy like his daddy too.

Something buzzed in my pocketbook.

Kisha stopped playing with her doll. "Grandma, isn't that your phone?"

"Oh, you right baby. That sure is."

I reached in and grabbed the ringing phone from my mammoth handbag.

"Hello."

"Mama. I wanted to call to tell you, Judy, the kids and I would be there in three hours."

"What?" Oh then I remembered. Junior mentioned he was bringing the family to visit. So much had happened in one week.

Before I could tell Junior about his sister, he rattled on about frying fish and firing up his dad's grill. That boy always had food on his mind. Seeing the condition I was facing now, Junior would have to be careful. We had heart disease and diabetes running its course in our family.

When that boy found out about his sister, my son's blood pressure would surely rise.

No need to give a person more than they could bite off and chew.

30

By the time we were back to the house, Leesa was off the hook and I had purchased several pounds of fish from the fish market.

Amos met us coming out of the car.

"Well, how did things go?"

I handed him a brown bag. "I think we are good. Still no idea about who killed Mary though. Do you mind helping me carry these into the house?"

"Sure." He peeked into the bag. "You got a lot of fish here, planning to have a fish fry."

"My son is coming and he has his mouth is ready for some good eating. Why don't you come join us, that is if you don't have nothing better to do? I could use some help."

I tell you I had to be losing my mind or just that audacious to invite a man over to my house. Ralph used to be the one to clean fish, so I was hoping Amos wouldn't mind helping. Quite frankly, I preferred not to touch them if I could get someone else to do so.

Amos grinned. "You got yourself a deal."

So, about forty minutes later, we're in the kitchen, me getting the cornmeal mix ready and Amos hanging out over my kitchen sink scraping scales from the fish.

I looked out the window and watched Kisha and Porgy running around. I was pleased to see Leesa holding Tyric.

The doorbell rang. Junior and his family were not due for another hour. I opened the door to find a neighbor.

I put on my best smile. "Carmen, how are you? Come on in."

The woman looked at me with concern. "How are you? Is everything okay?"

"Girl, it's a long story, but my daughter is back."

"She is?"

I had a thought as I examined Carmen's incredulous expression. "Why don't you come back in the kitchen? I will introduce you two."

I cleared my throat when I returned to the kitchen. Amos turned from the sink. He eyed me and then nodded at Carmen.

I opened the door and called out to Leesa.

"Yeah Mama, what is it?"

Carmen stared at Leesa, almost in awe. "Wow, you really are back?"

Leesa frowned, "Don't I know you from somewhere?"

Okay, this was what I was looking for. I glanced over at Amos and noticed he stopped scraping fish scales long enough to watch the interaction. I had a feeling we were thinking the same thing. Although for the life of me, I didn't see any motive that would lead to Carmen killing one neighbor and almost killing another.

"Yeah, I remember now." Leesa shook her head. "I saw you out with Cedric. Y'all still dating?"

"Dating?" Carmen and I squawked.

As Carmen and I stared at each other, a voice hollered into the kitchen. "Hey, what's going on back in there?"

Speaking of the devil, Cedric strolled in. All of us seemed frozen. Except for Kisha. She ran into her favorite uncle's arms.

Cedric lifted his niece up. "Hey boo! What's happening?"

Kisha giggled, "Uncle Ceddy, look Mama is here."

Cedric looked at Leesa, then turned and did a double take at Carmen. For a moment his eyes stopped on Amos who had promptly turned back around to the fish. Cedric's eyes stopped on me, and then he asked, "You got a party or something going on in here? I guess for the prodigal daughter."

Leesa threw her hands in the air and huffed. "What? I took a break okay. I did not ask all y'all to lose your minds."

Cedric placed Kisha on the floor and argued back with his sister. "You should have told Mama where you were going."

I held my hand to my head. "That's enough you two? You are adults!"

"Maybe I should be going?" Carmen made a move to leave the kitchen, but was blocked by a larger figure.

Despite his huge girth, my eldest child had quietly arrived and stood in the doorway observing all of us. Junior's voice boomed, "What's going on in here, folks?"

Behind my son, I saw my daughter-in-law peeking around Junior's shoulder. The twins squeezed into the kitchen, one on each side of their father. They headed straight to me.

"Grandma, grandma."

"Hey babies." I loved these boys, but even as I hugged them, my energy was zapped. They wiggled and giggled, ready to get into something.

"Who's that?"

I looked over at Junior, who frowned and stared in the direction of my kitchen sink. There Amos continued to stand, cleaning fish in the midst of the chaos my family had slung into my house.

In less than twelve hours my children and their children, some with questionable love interests had all assembled in my kitchen.

It was almost perfect.

Almost.

31

Junior glared at Amos and then turned questioning eyes on me. Amos didn't exactly volunteer, but I invited him and I wasn't about to take any mess from my eldest. I had enough dealing with my youngest this week.

"Ralph, Jr., I know I taught you better manners than that. You remember Mr. Amos Jones, my next door neighbor. He volunteered to help clean fish."

To keep from having to answer any further questions, I shooed the little ones and the men outside to the backyard. I'm sure it was a shock to both of my sons having another man around me. Certainly, my children didn't expect me to not move forward with life.

Not that I was looking for anything further with Amos. *Aren't we too old?*

After the chaos had settled a bit and everyone had eaten, Cora stopped by and joined me in the kitchen with the younger women, Leesa, Carmen and Judy.

As Cora fixed her plate, my daughter-in-law commented, "I can't remember the last time I cooked a meal."

Cora piped up, "What do you feed your husband and children? Child, you can't survive on McDonald's food, you know?"

I had to agree with Cora, but I couldn't talk. My two grandsons were on the chubby side the same way Junior was when he was their age. Unfortunately, the weight never seems to quite go away but increases the older you get.

Judy appeared to be tired. "With those two rascals out there, just to get them settled down so I can cook is a chore. I hate to admit it, but I feel like such a failure as a mom when it comes to feeding my kids."

Leesa joined in, "Kisha can be such a picky eater. Now I have two mouths to feed. At least you have my brother to help you."

Judy rolled her eyes. "Your brother is not much help."

I glanced over at Judy. Junior was starting to sound like his late father. I cleared my throat. "Well, I had my two sons, two years apart mind you. I was barely twenty-one when I learned how to crank out all those meals. I can understand where you are coming from, but we have to pay attention to what the kids are eating." Then, I smiled. "You know Leesa, remember when Mary's family and ours would trade nights?"

Leesa smiled. "Yeah, I remember. I would sit with Jennifer and talk outside. Mr. Fleming made the best burgers. So much has changed."

There was a bit of silence as Leesa and I reminisced. Carmen and Judy seemed to understand what we were thinking.

Leesa leaned forward on the table. "Mama, who do you think killed Mary? I still can't believe all the Flemings are gone. Just like Dad."

"Not gone for good honey." I knew Leesa still struggled a bit with her faith. "You know we will see them all again. I have been trying to figure out who would harm Mary."

Cora chimed in, "Sounds like the biggest issue is motive, because you said she wasn't robbed."

"That's awful." Judy shook her head.

I had noticed for about thirty minutes Judy rubbed her belly quite a bit.

"Judy. Is there something you need to tell me?"

Her eyes grew wide. "What do you mean?"

I didn't want any more surprises and I had a sneaky feeling Judy wasn't tired just from the three-hour drive. I sighed, "So when you due?"

"How did you know I was pregnant?"

"Just a guess. Believe me." I glanced at Leesa. "I don't always figure these things out."

Leesa grinned sheepishly. "This is great. Tyric will have someone close to his age. Do you know what it is?"

Judy shifted in her seat uncomfortably. "No. To be honest I just found out a few days ago. I've been tired, but I didn't think it was... anyway I haven't told Junior. So you can't say anything."

What is with this family and secrets?

"Well, you can't keep that type of information for too long."

"Wow, that's wonderful. I can tell all of you really love your children," Carmen commented as her bright face turned red around the cheeks.

I'd almost forgotten Carmen was in the kitchen. She'd been so quiet. The way she sat in the chair reminded me of the time I saw her in the hospital cafeteria with the head-phones in her ears. Carmen's eyes had begun to water. "Honey, you okay?"

"I'm fine. Sorry. Don't mind me. I really like your family, Mrs. Patterson. Growing up, my family moved around a lot. Then when I was about thirteen I found out I was adopted. I've no doubt they loved me, but I always wondered about my birth mother."

"Have you ever thought about looking for her?"

"I did once, but I saw how it bothered my adoptive mother so much, I stopped."

The things you don't know about folks. I looked at Carmen, examining her face, now that I know she was adopted. I'm not sure why, but the spirit stirred inside me. I did tend to fly off the handle thinking the worst of people when I didn't quite understand. This woman might be what my Cedric needed in his life.

My thoughts were interrupted by squealing and yapping. Kisha and Porgy burst through the kitchen door. "Okay, you two take it outside. That dog is not to be in my kitchen."

Judy asked, "Eugeena, when did you get a dog?"

"It's my neighbor Mary's dog. I felt sorry for the poor thing after ... finding her. Besides he makes good company."

As I guzzled down the rest of my iced tea, my mind fixated on one thought. The night of her death, Mary hadn't brought the dog back in. What would have caused her to leave Porgy outside? Maybe the person who came by the house that day really didn't like dogs. But Mary could have left the dog in another room. Was Mary outside when the visitor came by?

"Mama, you okay?" Leesa nudged my elbow, interrupting my thoughts.

"I'm fine. Just thinking." If only the little four-legged creature could talk. He would be what this case really needed. A solid witness.

32

Sunday morning was quiet despite the fact that I had a house full of people. Porgy managed to make his way on the bed again and I didn't move him. My daughter was scot-free and sleeping safely down the hall, but a crime had been committed. There were too many unanswered questions.

Maybe Mary's house was about to be burglarized and she surprised the thief. The thief killed her and then decided it wasn't worth taking anything. It would have been real easy to leave a fingerprint or fibers somewhere for the cops to pick up on.

No longer wanting to look at the ceiling, I decided to start breakfast. I didn't know if I could round up everyone for church later in the morning, but breakfast may help.

Porgy beat me into the kitchen. I filled up his bowl and set fresh water down. Filling up a coffee pot with fresh water, I decided it would be good idea to introduce my baked cheese grits to the rest of the family.

As picky as Kisha was about eating, she seemed to like the grits. Then again she was like her grandmother; anything with cheese was alright with her.

An apron lay across one of the kitchen chairs. It was the one I gave Amos to wear yesterday to protect his clothes. I guess that's why Junior had such a strong reaction since it was his father's apron.

I'm still not sure what all happened yesterday. It been awhile since I'd had my entire family together. God answered many prayers of mine in one swoop. I blinked in order to keep the rush of tears that flowed into my eyes from falling down my face. It didn't work. I heaved and then wiped my wet face.

Thank you, Lord, for your grace and mercy. You are so good to me and I know I don't deserve it.

I heard a noise behind me. My eyes met my firstborn son. "Junior, what you doing up so early?"

"I could ask you the same thing. Kind of early to be starting breakfast."

"There's a lot of people in this house. Even Cedric stayed over last night. Want some coffee for starters?"

"Sure!" Junior pulled out a chair from the table and sat down. "So you and Mr. Amos an item?"

Now my hand wasn't wet, but the coffee cup I grabbed from the cabinet went sliding and then crashed to the floor. "Not that cup." The large mug had been with me for years. In fact it was a past Christmas gift from Mary, at least ten years old. Why did I suddenly recognize all these memories of Mary? She seemed so much a part of my life and other times, a distant memory.

I missed her more than I ever thought I would.

Junior jumped up and grabbed the broom from the closet. "I'll get it."

I pulled down another cup and poured the brewed coffee. Porgy came over to inspect the pieces on the floor with his nose. "No, you don't. Come here."

I picked up the dog that covered my face with what must be doggie kisses. I didn't quite have that in mind. "Okay, you. That is not necessary. You are a little mess."

"You are really keeping that dog?"

"Of course I am. I like animals. Your dad didn't like them at least not in the house. Porgy here will make good company."

"I guess it wouldn't hurt to have a watch dog." Junior swept up the remains of the cup and after he emptied the shards he added quietly, "And you have Amos?"

"Excuse me." *I am not interested in Amos and even if I was I surely wasn't discussing my love life with my son.*

"I'm just saying, he's a nice guy. We had some great conversations yesterday. He seemed real keen on you."

I stopped petting Porgy at this point. "What does that mean?"

"He helped you look for Leesa. Wants to solve who killed Mary."

"He is a former detective, which I appreciate. A very helpful neighbor." I emphasized neighbor as I looked at my son. "He does cut the grass for me. Cedric never seems to have time to get over here."

"Must make you feel good to have a man looking after you."

I frowned. What was wrong with the boy? That kind of talk I expected from Cedric, even Leesa, not Junior. "Son, are you okay?"

Junior sighed and then took another slurp of coffee. "I guess it didn't hit me until last night, being back in the house." He continued, "It just kind of put me at-ease some, that you had a decent neighbor especially with what happened to Louise. You didn't tell me about her being attacked the other night." His voice turned accusatory.

Louise. My dear friend. I didn't get to go by the hospital to see her with all the excitement of Leesa's return."You know I need to get to the hospital and see Louise. Did you know her son, William, is in town?"

"Really, I hadn't seen him in years. What's he up to now?"

"I have no idea, but the last time he spoke he was threatening to put Louise in a nursing home. I don't know if I would like that at all."

"People have to do what they need to do to protect the folks they love, Mom."

"Yeah, well he could have thought about visiting his mother more. That woman pined away over him."

Why did William just show back up in town out of the blue? That slipped my mind too. He came back just as his mother was brutally attacked. I let it go and concentrated on the meal. Soon the rest of the family woke up and to my delight everyone attended church.

The Brown twins stared and I grinned back. I was a proud mama this morning and really didn't care what they were thinking.

Back at the house as I watched my family laughing and talking my thoughts turned to Louise. I needed to go see her. When Louise woke up she could surely send the police in the right direction. If she's lucid enough, she could possibly help them sketch out the suspect.

Then another thought sent my heart pounding. Who's to say Louise was completely out of danger now. Someone might not be too happy about Louise waking up.

33

I sprinted through the hospital door. Had the police even considered Louise was in the hospital because someone intended to kill her? It was imperative to find Louise's attacker, who I'm pretty sure had to be the same person who murdered Mary.

Sitting in my own kitchen in the morning, it occurred to me both of these women were attacked in their kitchens. Did Mary's murderer attack Louise with similar intentions? But why? And who was this person both of my neighbors so willingly let into their home?

I entered the elevator almost bumping into a family. It appeared to be an older woman flanked by her two daughters, one on each side. As the elevator doors closed, one of the young women reached out and held down the open elevator button. I'm not sure what went on between them, but with some coaxing the two women seemed to convince the older woman she had to leave the elevator. As they walked out, the older woman turned her head, catching my eyes. There was a deep sadness there, like she'd lost her best friend.

The elevator beeped as it passed a floor finally arriving on the sixth floor, intensive care. I scanned the hallway area and the small waiting room. As far as I could tell, William wasn't anywhere to be seen, which was just fine with me. I didn't want to run into him because I would have to tell that boy, I mean man, how I really feel about him sticking his mother in a nursing home. I knew it was none of my business and not my decision to make. Louise was doing just fine.

I rounded the corner and headed towards a door. I pressed the button setting off a buzz from the other side. A second later, a voice said, "Yes, who would you like to see?"

"Louise Hopkins." A longer buzz produced a click in the door latch. The heavy wide door swished as it opened.

A nurse greeted me, "What's the relation?"

"Next door neighbor. How is she?"

The nurse ignored my question. "Your name?"

"Eugeena Patterson, I was here the other night."

The woman scanned a list. "I have your name listed. You have fifteen minutes with her." She pointed to the room. "Her condition is stabilized, but she is still heavily medicated. As you know with her age, we need to keep her comfortable and keep a close eye on her recovery."

I nodded. "Thank you for the report." The image that met me as I entered the room was slightly better than Friday night. Louise looked so frail, her head framed by her white halo of hair. As she lay with equipment beeping around her, her wrinkles seemed to have deepened and her cheeks more hollow. Something about hospitals added ten or more years on a person.

I pulled up the chair and sat down. As I gazed at her face, I noted the bruising around her temple, once very purplish, now faded. An IV snaked from around her arm up to the pouch hanging on a hook. Her attacker hit Louise across her head. *Could my old friend recover from this injury?*

I sure wanted to see her eyes open. But maybe that was a good thing at least for now. Whoever did this knew as long as Louise couldn't talk, they couldn't be identified.

I couldn't wrap my head around who would hurt either woman. But something happened to provoke an insane rage. The attacker grabbed whatever he or she could get their hand on and proceeded to cause damage. To human life.

I looked up at the clock on the wall. Where was William? It was still kind of strange to me he showed up out of the blue. And just when something bad happened to his mother.

Louise always tried to highlight the good things that William did, but most people knew that William had a tendency to do all the wrong things. In the late eighties and early nineties before he took off across the United States, Louise had to keep an eye on her pocketbook and her possessions to ensure her own son wouldn't walk off with them to support his drug habit.

The more I thought about it, the more I started to wonder was William involved in this somehow. It seemed like Louise would've mentioned if he was back in town. She was just as lonely for family as I was, even more so with William being her only living child and rarely visiting. Suppose all the time William was the one who committed robberies in the neighborhood that he knew so well. He certainly knew Mary.

Mary would not just let him into the house. Before she lost her family, she was the kind of person that always tried to see the good in people. Unlike me, I was always suspicious or overly cautious. Mary became such a recluse in recent years; I imagined she would have been more cautious especially knowing William's history.

But Mary reached out to Leesa. Which made me wonder, who was the person purposely trying to mislead the police by implicating my daughter as a suspect?

I looked at Louise. Suppose she was protecting her son all that time. How many times did Louise inquire about Leesa?

Wait a minute stop all this, Eugeena. First of all, this is Louise we are talking about here. The one who couldn't keep her mouth closed.

No, if Louise knew something she would have told me. This whole thing was making me crazy. I even wondered about Amos. Everyone seemed to be a suspect.

A noise startled me. I expected to see the nurse, but all I saw was a flash of white clothing. That's weird. Most nurses just walked right in while you're visiting and do whatever they have to do.

I got up from my chair and headed towards the intensive care desk area. The same nurse who greeted me when I came in was busily tapping on a computer keyboard.

She looked up when I leaned over the desk. "Was someone just at the door now?"

The woman peered over her glasses at me. "Yes, but I told her only one person allowed in the room at the time." The nurse shrugged, "I guess she was concerned about her grandmother."

Grandmother? I decided to keep my mouth closed. What I knew that the nurse didn't know was that Louise didn't have any grandchildren. That is unless William had a few surprises on the side. "I hate to bother you but can you describe her?"

The nurse described the woman and then frowned, "Why all the questions?"

"You do know Mrs. Hopkins is in intensive care because someone attacked her?"

"I'm familiar with her situation."

"Then you should also know her attacker hasn't been found."

"Well, you don't think ..."

I looked at the woman like she'd lost her mind.

"Now that I think about it, she was acting nervously."

"Call the police. Tell them someone needs to be here looking after Mrs. Hopkins." I stormed out the door into the waiting area and drove like a mad woman back toward Sugar Creek. How did I miss this? None of it made any sense.

Grown folks talking, children screaming and a dog barking in delight were the sounds that met me as I entered the house. On the way home, I had cooked up a plan and Porgy was going to help me, but first I needed to talk to Amos.

"Mama, is that you? How's Louise doing?" Junior called out.

"She's still in intensive ... what are you doing here? And you?"

Amos and Wayne sat across from both of my boys; all had cards in their hands. "Junior asked me if I knew how to play spades. Couldn't resist. I hadn't played in years. I needed a partner. Wayne here was available."

Wayne, still looking clean-cut, grinned. "Hey Miss Eugeena. Like old times."

Maybe that was my imagination, but my two sons seemed to have taken to Amos. Wayne seemed to look upon the man as a father figure in the past few days too. I couldn't sit and ponder that for long, I was on a mission.

"Louise still hasn't woken up enough to talk."

Amos looked thoughtful. "That might be a good thing for now. Police still need to catch who attacked her."

He was so right about that, but I didn't know if I could interrupt their game and pull Amos to the side to tell him what I knew.

So, I continued with Plan A, not even quite sure of the full plan. I went off to find my four-legged roommate. "Porgy, you ready to go for a walk?" The dog started bouncing around as soon as he saw the leash. I snapped it on his little collar. I headed back down the stairs to see the men folks were still tied up with their game. Amos eyed me. "You're going for a walk this time of day?"

I stared blankly. Did he know what I was up to? "Porgy's been cooped up for a while."

"Still, it's really warm out."

Junior and Cedric were both looking at their cards, but I could tell their ears were cocked to our conversation.

"Oh I will be fine. Porgy and I will take a little walk and we will be right back." I emphasized right back and looked at Amos. I didn't want to come right out and say I suspect one of our neighbors had been hiding something. "If I don't come back, call in the troops." Amos stared at me. I know my smile was wobbly. I'm not good at hiding things. Hiding was just as bad as lying to me. In the case of what I was about to do, I figured it might be a good idea to drop some clues.

I shut the front door behind me and headed down my driveway in the direction of Mary's house. As I walked, Porgy panted and trotted along my side, he didn't seem as chipper, maybe because he was nearing his old home. As I passed the array of snapdragons and lilies, a picture started to come together in my mind. How did I miss this?

34

The garden. Until today, I never noticed the small garden on the side of the house. Could have been a coincidence, but the flowers looked like "children" from Mary's garden.

Tamara answered the door. She looked like she needed a good night's sleep. "Mrs. Patterson?"

Porgy lurched forward on the leash so hard he almost yanked my shoulder out the socket. I pulled the little Corgi back.

Tamara grabbed the door. "What's going on?"

"Porgy, calm down. What's wrong with you?" I'd never seen the dog react quite that way to anybody. He seemed pretty friendly to almost everyone. Did he react this way before to Tamara? "I'm sorry. He's been cooped up in the house. I don't know what's got into the little fellow."

I bent down and picked the dog up into my arms. "Do you mind if we come in?"

"You want me to let that thing into my house? Suppose he attacks me."

Porgy growled. My little furry friend was definitely trying to tell me something. He clearly didn't like Tamara. All those times that Tamara was over, Porgy had been trying to tell me something. I looked at this woman who had been in my house. My kitchen.

Mary's body was in her kitchen. Louise was attacked in her kitchen.

"You have some beautiful flowers." I petted Porgy's head, hoping to sooth his nerves, but his little muscles were tight with tension. So were mine. I continued blabbing. "Looks like you have some of Mary's favorites. Did she give you some gardening tips? I know she tried to help me learn. I was a lost cause."

Tamara cleared her throat and gazed at me, well mostly at Porgy, "Miss Eugeena, can I help you?"

"I wanted to check on you. I haven't seen you in a few days."

Tamara's face crumbled, but she regained her composure. "Thanks for taking the time to check on me."

"Honey, are you okay?" I did feel for this lonely young woman.

"My husband left. Just like everyone does. They all leave."

Porgy whimpered. Right then and there, I should have walked off. But I couldn't. I moved the small dog to under my arm. "I'm sorry to hear, honey. Why don't you come over, we've got plenty of food at my house. My whole family came in this weekend."

"No, no thanks. I wouldn't want to barge in on you. I guess everyone is upset about Leesa."

Leesa. Tamara doesn't know Leesa is back.

I needed to get that girl closer to Amos. And away from her home. My pitiful plan had already fizzled.

"You sure you don't want to come over. I don't want you to be by yourself."

"I appreciate it, Miss Eugeena, but that's exactly-" her voice caught for a second. Then she swallowed. "I need to be by myself for awhile."

"No, Tamara, I insist. I don't tell many people this, but my marriage wasn't all that great for several years. Honey, the Lord can work it out."

Tamara's eyes flooded with tears. "I don't think God can fix this. It's too late."

"Okay, if you don't come over, I'm going to bring the feast to you." *I planned to bring back Amos.*

She stared at me for a few minutes, like she heard me speak my plan out loud. "I appreciate you being so kind. All of you have been kind to me."

"All of us?" I responded. Before I could think, I inquired, "Mary and Louise too?"

Tamara's eyes grew wide, and then narrowed with a deep anger. "What did you say?"

Too late to turn back now. "That night when you went to see Mary. What happened?"

"What are you talking about? I didn't go to see Mary."

"Are you sure? You sure you didn't make friends with your neighbor across the street? Maybe you were angry and something terrible happened." I couldn't seem to stop interrogating the woman.

Tamara's body trembled. Her fists tightened. Her small stature seemed to shrink before my eyes. "You can't prove anything."

My stomach was churning on the inside. *Good Lord! Was that a confession?* All the time Porgy whimpered. I placed him on the ground and let the leash slip from my hand. That dog took off down the street. I turned to head after him, but heard Tamara squeal "No!" behind me.

Then I heard a click.

I watched Porgy's little body getting smaller and smaller. I hope with all my heart he would have sense enough to head toward the house he'd called home for only a week.

I turned to Tamara and put on my meanest look.

"Look, you are in enough trouble already."

Her hand holding the gun trembled. She hissed, "Get in here. We don't want to attract attention from the neighbors." As I glided past Tamara into her house, my thoughts flashed to what a good time I had with my family and how they may never see me alive again.

35

Tamara shoved me towards the couch. "Sit down over there so I can think."

Lord knows if that child didn't have that gun, I would've backhanded her. Better yet, if the Lord had given humans the ability to kill by looking at somebody, Miss Tamara would have been one dead chick right now.

I sat down, not taking my eyes off Tamara. I exhaled, "I can't believe I trusted you and let you into my home. Looks like you made a fool out of me. Chile, what is your problem?"

Tamara paced back and forth. "I didn't mean to become friends. I liked Mary. It was an accident. It really was ... she fell. Louise and you. All of you took me under your wings."

She fell. Or was she pushed? I opened my mouth to ask the questions racing through my head. "Chile, why didn't you call for help?"

Tamara shrugged. "I don't know maybe because I had no business being there."

The doorbell rang before I could inquire about what Tamara meant. Tamara pointed the gun in my direction and placed her finger against her lips.

I don't know who was at the door, but I hoped God sent the cavalry after me. I leaned forward as Tamara opened the door. Too bad the couch was positioned behind the door.

"Hey Tamara, how are you? I was wondering if you've seen Eugeena. Porgy came back without her. Her family is out searching for her. You know she has diabetes."

Amos! Praise God for that little furry wonder dog. He did head back to the house. Oh I wasn't going to complain about him sleeping on the bed ever again.

Tamara's voice oozed with sugary sweetness, "No, I haven't seen her."

I opened my mouth to protest, but then I remembered the gun behind Tamara's back. I certainly didn't want harm to come to Amos.

I swallowed and prayed. *Lord Jesus, I don't know what's going on here. You taught us how to be a good neighbor. I'm not the best neighbor, but I reached out to this woman. I trust you and your plan right now.*

I shifted in my seat and tried to see if I could catch Amos' attention.

"Why don't you join us out here? We could use all the help we can get. I know how special Eugeena is to you," Amos coaxed Tamara.

The woman stuttered her reply. "Well, I'm kind of in a jam right now. I'm sure Miss Eugeena will be back soon. She probably just walked a little farther and Porgy being difficult just ran off. She's probably looking for him."

There was a moment of silence. Amos must have been thinking about what Tamara said. Finally he spoke, "You're right, she could be out looking for the dog. Well, I will let you know when she's back."

"Okay. I hope you find her."

Tamara closed the door, but something blocked her from closing it all the way. "What?" The woman swung the door open and pointed the gun towards Amos.

I yelled, "No, don't you dare."

I placed my hands against my face and watched in horror as Amos lunged forward to grab Tamara's arms.

An explosion of noise from the gun caused me to throw my heavy body to the floor. On all fours I crawled as fast as I could to the back of a nearby chair. Screaming radiated in my ears.

Wait that was me screaming.

I shut my mouth and listened to Tamara crying hysterically now. "No, let me go. I didn't mean to do it."

Then, a voice from above me said, "Eugeena, you alright?"

I pulled my arms from where I had them wrapped tight around my head and looked up into a face I'd come to enjoy seeing. "You're okay. What happened?"

Amos reached down and I took his hand. He pulled me up from the floor in one swoop. Pretty strong for an old guy too. He asked me. "Are you okay?"

I looked over to where Tamara was on the floor. One cop was placing her in handcuffs, while another one watched.

The cops were here. I turned to Amos and grinned, "How did you know?"

"When people start acting strange and out of character, that's a sure sign to pay attention. When you came back from visiting Louise, you seemed uptight about the experience and on a mission. Plus the Eugeena I know ain't walking in hot weather anywhere. As soon as you left, I excused myself from the game, called in a favor and then I followed you."

"You followed me," I said incredulously. I laughed and reached over to hug my bald-headed neighbor. To my surprise, he squeezed back.

I really liked my next door neighbor Amos Jones. I believe the feelings were mutual.

Epilogue

My family crowded me for hours. After we all knew Tamara was tucked away behind bars, most of my family started to travel back home. Only Amos, Leesa, her children and I remained at the house. We sat on the porch, occasionally looking down the street at what had almost become my crime scene.

Tamara was a con woman. She played the whole neighborhood. When her house was searched, she'd been quite the thief. Her game was to get to know people and find out their habits so she could rob their house. *Life of an idle housewife!*

What wasn't clear is whether Tamara's husband caught on to her "illegal" shopping? Was that why the man left?

Leesa's eyes were red. I patted my baby girl's leg. "Honey, you didn't know. I let that child into my home. Mary and Louise did the same thing, not knowing she might have been setting us up to rob us blind later."

Leesa shook her head. "Mama, I still don't know why she killed Mary and then tried to pin her crime on me."

Amos spoke up. "Leesa, you were a convenience for her. Mary rarely left the house except to do shopping but when she did it was like clockwork. Same time every Friday."

217

Leesa nodded, "That's why Mary kept looking at the clock because she wanted to stick to her schedule."

I added, "Right. Poor thing probably put her groceries away, let Porgy outside and fixed herself a glass of water, not knowing that Tamara was hiding in her house. Tamara must have thought she could sneak in and get out before Mary returned."

Leesa frowned. "So Mary caught this crazy woman in her house and was killed."

That's as best we could figure. Louise was awake, but she didn't seem to remember anything about the night she was attacked. There were two coffee mugs on the counter so I felt like Louise figured something out before we all did. Poor old woman just about lost her life.

I shuddered. I'd almost walked through death's door myself.

Leesa stood, "I'm going to put the kids in the bed. See you later, Mr. Amos."

After Leesa went inside, I turned to Amos. "I can't say thank you enough. You saved my life today."

He grinned, "Next time remember to include a professional in your plan."

"I tried to drop as many hints to you as I could."

It could have been the light sparkling in Amos' eyes, but his face beamed. "Yeah, you did. Not bad for an amateur."

I grinned and then guzzled down my iced tea. Yep. Whatever came next, Detective Eugeena Patterson would be on the scene.

About the Author

Tyora Moody is an author and entrepreneur. Tyora has coined her books as Soul-Searching Suspense. *Deep Fried Trouble* is the first book in the Eugeena Patterson Mystery series.

Tyora is also the author of the Victory Gospel Series (*When Rain Falls* and *When Memories Fade*). The third and final book in the series, *When Perfection Fails*, will be released March 2014.

She is a member of Sisters in Crime and American Christian Fiction Writers. She served as a judge for the Christy Awards for three years.

You can visit her online at **TyoraMoody.com**. For more about the character Eugeena, visit her blog at **EugeenaPatterson.com**.

Shattered Dreams:
A Short Story

In this prequel short story, Eugeena Patterson has always been the glue keeping her fragmented family together. Will her troubled teenage daughter rip the family apart?

Other Books
by Tyora Moody

Victory Gospel Series

When Rain Falls, Book 1 (In Stores Now)
When Memories Fade, Book 2 (In Stores Now)
When Perfection Fails, Book 3 (March 2014)

CPSIA information can be obtained
at www.ICGtesting.com
Printed in the USA
LVHW020446290422
717484LV00010B/888

9 780989 415309